Primal Passion

BY

Eidahs

COVER ART BY

KEMVEE

BINKY INK

THE LITERARY ARM OF BINKY PRODUCTIONS

WWW.BINKYPRODUCTIONS.COM/PRIMALPASSION

Published in 2025 by Binky Ink
Cover & Portrait Art by Kemvee
Editing by Binky Ink
Latin Verification by Cat

ISBN: 978-1-0692305-8-4

<u>WARNINGS:</u>

Strong Language, Mature Sexual Subject Matter,

Violence, Blood, Smoking.

Primal Passion is the second book in the *Tenebrarum*

chronology, an ongoing series of

Supernatural LGBTQ Erotic Romance Thriller books.

Primal Passion
James Sharpe

Primal Passion
Chad Sharpe

Table of Contents

Prologue 9
Chapter One 18
Chapter Two 38
Chapter Three 59
Chapter Four 75
Chapter Five 88
Chapter Six 102
Chapter Seven 116
Chapter Eight 131
Chapter Nine 149
Chapter Ten 172
Chapter Eleven 188
Chapter Twelve 204
Chapter Thirteen 228
Epilogue 252
More To Come 269
Acknowledgements 271
Also By Eidahs 273
About the Author 274

PROLOGUE

The sky shifted from dark to mellow as the first signs of morning appeared. Chad stood on the edge of the river, staring out at the horizon and chancing fate as he sometimes did.

Once, he had stood by the water every morning to watch the sunrise when he was still human. Once, he had been able to appreciate the sun. He would stand with his eyes closed, facing the sun, and feel its warmth on his face, and smile. Now, as a vampire, such an indulgence would burn his face and weaken him. Be that as it may, Chad often came here and tested his limits so he could see the beginnings of the sunrise.

His aching heart tormented him. The cool wind blowing through his curly hair and the goosebumps rising on his taupe skin did nothing to quell the ache. Only watching the first rays of light appear before he'd dash to return home somehow made him forget it.

Someone somewhere was listening to Gregorian chanting. It brought Chad back to the days when vampires and werewolves were once allied, like now, wanting to set aside past feuds between the two peoples. The 17th century was the height of Baroque music, yet some beings of the Underworld had brought back the medieval chanting as their form of dominance, led by a group of insurgents who wanted nothing to do with such an alliance.

These vampires killed werewolves, and the were-wolves killed vampires in turn. Then they manipulated the fae people into outright war with the vampire kind. These vampires were purists, wanting nothing to taint their blood, wanting only to be the dominant kind of the Underworld and to never mix with werewolves or fae.

It was a brutal time in history for vampires, as the fae retaliated tenfold before they learnt the truth. The fae confessed their error and immediately vowed friend-ship with the vampires, but Chad had known then his people would be too resentful, for the damage done was too great.

The fae were exiled from the tangible realm, the Upper Realm, and were ordered to remain in their magical Fae Realm unless specifically requested to step out. Since then, the fae people have been seldom seen in the human realm.

The music grew louder, it resonated, as a fine line of faint light rose to meet the horizon.

Chad thought back to when the new alliance between vampires and werewolves was first proposed over a year ago. Tension had risen to critical levels, but it could have been far worse. He remembered seeing James for the first time and feeling that pang in his heart that told him he'd fall for him and fear losing him for years to come. Despite his warnings, he still pursued him and took that risk, the risk of fear greater than the possibilities themselves.

Chad closed his eyes. It still hurt, remembering everyone he had already loved and lost. Still, he was content, or he believed he should be.

His thoughts brought him to the first kiss he shared with James.

* * *

Chad held James's hands in his, staring into his brown eyes as they sat on the loveseat in the guest bedroom of Rachel's home. Chad could practically feel James's heart pounding just as fast as his, as though it were in his own chest. The hair on James's tawny muscular pecs was as meticulously groomed as ever, even after a night of fighting, though his shoulder-length hair was tousled, giving the werewolf a wild look.

'I've never been with a werewolf before,' Chad admitted.

'I've never considered or wanted to be with a vampire before,' said James. 'Admittedly, I flirted with Liam, but I thought he was human. You are the first vampire to truly captivate my attention, Chad.' James looked down. 'If we are together . . . I am to be the pack's Alpha.' He chuckled nervously. 'I'm more nervous at the prospect of coming out as a vampire-lover than I was when I first came out as bisexual.'

Chad placed his hand under James's chin and gently tilted the werewolf's face up to meet his eyes.

'James.' Chad recognised the passion he felt towards the werewolf. 'I am ready to face whatever we might face if it means I can be with you.'

James lunged forward, capturing Chad's lips in a kiss that took his breath away. Chad returned the urgent kiss with a feverish moan. He and James clawed at each other as they made out, wanting to explore every inch of each other's bodies all at once.

* * *

Chad allowed himself a smile. The wait to be alone for proper intimacy after being interrupted from that kiss had been more than Chad thought he could manage. They had broken Rachel's rule and made love the following night. Attempting to be as quiet as possible, they had gone very slowly, which had only amplified all sensations. Not to mention Chad had discovered how true it was that a werewolf's naturally rough tongue could induce so much pleasure.

James was Chad's first and only werewolf, and the experience was so much more exhilarating than Chad could have anticipated. The natural roughness of a werewolf's tongue amplified all sensation felt, and it always made Chad's pleasure mount tenfold.

James had discovered Chad's preference quickly as they explored every inch of their bare skin. James had requested with so much desire, 'Can I get behind—?' And Chad had interrupted with an anticipatory whimper of need, 'Please!' James had lain down on top of Chad as Chad lay on his stomach. It was like no other sexual experience Chad had lived, so filled with emotions he had yearned to feel for so long. The two had shouted out into the same pillow, attempting to stifle their screams as they dripped with sweat onto each other.

A wave of elation hit Chad at the memory and heat rose to his face. He smiled.

The Sharpe pack welcomed and accepted Chad with open arms, especially after everything that had gone down. The pack comprised many families and extended families – it was indeed one of the most powerful and largest packs on the continent. All of them accepted that a vampire might be the Partner-Alpha, and Chad was ready to take a vow to the responsibilities that would come with it, while still remaining loyal to his vampire coven.

While the other elders and the leaders of the coven rebuilt their manor, albeit a different manor, and established new safehouses, Chad wanted to remain close to his new friends. He wanted to teach and look after Liam. The young vampire had so much promise, not just because of his unique abilities, but as a fresh vampire too. And Liam had wanted to be close to his sister to help with the baby. So they all bought a house together, a large mansion, and they had all pitched in equally on the mortgage.

Chad chuckled. It was strange, perhaps, but it was nice. They had a common living room and kitchen, and many other common rooms they could relax in together, separate bedrooms with separate sitting rooms for privacy. Each bedroom was like a private suite with its own ensuite utilities, but the common areas were where they spent most of their time. It felt like Chad's own little coven.

Chad's wedding to James had been a small, quaint affair, compared to what James initially wanted it to be, and it was a much cherished moment. They had invited the pack for a party beforehand to celebrate, and the werewolves understood that their Alpha and his vamp wanted the ceremony to be more private and calm. So in the end, they had both, marrying each other in beautiful nightly winter empyrean. And his wedding photos showed his flaring eyes as white as the snow.

Up until now, in all his millennia of existence, Chad had never married. He had been bound through ceremonial union of love as a human, but never before as a vampire. It was still strange to be promised to one only. It was spring now, and Chad and James were still navigating uncharted waters as newlyweds, even while having been a couple for over a year. It was amazing to Chad to realise how much he loved James – every time – how he was with a werewolf of all beings.

Chad had once dated a fae, but aside from that one lover, all others had been vampires. And yet, now, not only did he love a werewolf, but he had committed to him solely, had agreed to monogamy for him – had wanted it – and had wanted to marry him so much that he proposed the night James declared he was willing to leave the pack for him.

* * *

'My pack will just have no choice but to accept that their future Alpha is with a vampire,' insisted James. 'I'm ready to leave the pack for you. Chad, baby . . . I'm not losing you. I know what I feel.' He took Chad's hand and placed it on his heart. 'I'm not going to let the wars of our ancestors keep us apart.'

'That's actually really romantic, you know that?' Chad's lips curled into a smile on the side of his mouth. He sobered again. 'Everything that's happened made me realise that I won't let anything keep us apart either. Whatever happens, it happens to us together. I love you, James.'

'I love you, Chad.'

The two men kissed, their passion growing by the minute. The world narrowed and Chad's focus zeroed in on James as though everything around them no longer existed, and the only thing that mattered to Chad . . . was James and the love this werewolf had for him.

After making out for a while, knowing they would have to find shelter soon, for day was approaching fast, Chad needed to express his true desires. He knew then that he wanted to promise himself to James and James alone.

Chad took James's hands in his and locked his gaze on him. Never looking away, Chad slowly knelt on one knee. Looking up into James's piercing brown eyes, the intensity of their growing passion reflected in them, Chad asked, 'James Sharpe, my lover, my werewolf . . . will you marry me?'

He held his breath, waiting for the whispered answer James sobbed. 'Yes. Yes, I will, Chad, my lover, my vampire.'

Chad let out a sobbed laugh, grinning madly at James. He rose to his feet – still his eyes never left James.

Chad whispered, his voice husky. 'Then let me dash us to a safe place where we can celebrate our engagement properly and in privacy.'

James was devouring him before Chad had even finished voicing the desire, and their passion had entwined them that morning, as it continued to do so every day they spent loving each other.

* * *

Something drew Chad's attention in his periphery. Chad turned his gaze to a group of people afar, walking along the river's edge amidst the trees. They wore black cloaks, and Chad realised they were the ones chanting. Chad used his vampiric sight to focus on the newcomers.

One of them turned and Chad saw the back of the hood. A chill ran up Chad's spine. The emblem on the cloak was the very symbol of that long-dead faction of vampires – a sun cross with an incongruent lozenge in the centre that represented a spearhead.

'It's just a coincidence,' he thought aloud.

He was a vampire, standing here, very close to being exposed to the morning sun, waiting for the rush of adrenaline to hit him when he would dash home and make it just in time before he would even begin to weaken. These people were walking and sitting down on the rocks – they were just arriving. They were not vampires.

One of them held a large leatherbound book. Chad figured them to be cosplayers and he chalked his dread up to memories.

As the voices swelled, Chad became aware of their words. Strange, their chanting did not comprise the typical *Lorem Ipsum* used by roleplayers. Chad focused on the lyrics of the chant.

Morte quam inferimus inimicis,
Pūritās restituētur,
Tenebrārum inferos dominabimur.

Through the Death we bring to our foes, purity is regained. We shall rule the Underworld.

Chad stood frozen in place. But these were not vampires, he could tell that much. Then were they—? He had rather not think about it. No, they were merely cosplayers who took their roles seriously, nothing more.

A glint of sunlight emerged and it was time to leave the riverbend.

CHAPTER ONE

Lounging in the loveseat, an arm around Chad's shoulders, James was enjoying the afternoon in the company of his vampire friends. Liam and Julian sat in different armchairs right beside them, legs extended enough to be playing footsie as they joked with James and Chad.

While they kept most windows well blocked with heavy drapes to keep the sunshine out, James liked that Chad and the others would wake in the afternoon, even if they had to stay indoors. While the living room had a natural amber light about it at this time of day, the two vampire husbands still looked pale as ever, green and blue eyes looking luminescent in the dim room.

'Careful,' Chad warned with a laugh, 'you'll kick me if you're not prudent. Go play footsie elsewhere.'

'Aw,' Liam pouted, his long blond bangs falling forward to hide one of his eyes, 'you sure you don't want some of this foot action?' He grinned cheekily. '*Sui Generis Lamia* footsie.'

Chad snorted a laugh.

'I'd rather Chad keep his feet for me,' chuckled James, 'unless he uses them to kick your hind.'

'Ooh!' both Liam and Julian shouted jovially. Chad bowed his head and laughed in his fist.

'I'm with James,' chuckled Julian. 'I'm the only one who gets to play footsie with you, Liam. And you best remember that.'

It was Chad's and James's turn to 'Ooh' out a laugh.

Rachel's voice echoed from down the hall, an annoyed shout, as she waltzed into the room, her long ginger hair swaying. Despite her tired eyes, she looked radiant in her casual maternity jogging pants and sweats.

'Hey! Immortal husbands! Will you keep it down? I just put Hikaru to sleep.' She pointed at them. 'You wake him up, and then you're on getting-the-baby-back-to-sleep duty.'

'Sorry,' James said, suppressing a laugh.

'It's not funny.' Rachel tossed a bag of diapers at James. 'Here, you can be on poopy duty.'

'What!' James stared at her wide-eyed. 'But today's—.'

'No buts! You're under my roof—'

'*Our* roof,' James corrected, feeling a bit affronted. 'We all paid equal amounts for this house. Do I need to remind you who made the down payment?'

'I'm the one who sleeps in the *master* bedroom,' Rachel retorted, sticking her neck forward and looking triumphant.

'Because it's on the first floor and next to the baby's room and it's convenient!' exclaimed James 'Look, you might be the Lady of the House, but it's still *all our* house.'

'You're the one who chose to live with the baby's uncle,' Julian pointed out. Suppressing a laugh, he brushed a lock of his black hair behind his ear, and leaned back, folding his arms.

'What can we say, we like having the two of you around,' voiced Chad. He and Julian playfully tapped each other's arms, chuckling.

'And you agreed to all the rules we wrote down,' Liam reminded James, a devious smile playing on the side of his mouth.

'Will you all just . . .' James sighed. 'It's Feral Night today.'

'Right,' said Chad, looking dismayed. It meant James would have to leave the house for the whole night. James hated that he had to do that as much as Chad did.

'Are we night, though?' Rachel challenged with attitude, a hand on her hip. 'No.'

'Ok, here.' James stood. 'How about I be on grocery duty, the vampires can be on poopy duty, and you can go relax before Keisuke comes home from work.'

Rachel's face lit up. 'You know what, I like that. I'm going to take a hot bath.'

She turned and went straight to the main bathroom without another word.

'And she was intense *before* post-pregnancy hormones,' muttered Chad.

Liam playfully slapped his arm. 'Watch what you say about my sister.' The two stifled a laugh, snorting in their throats.

James placed the bag of diapers in Liam's lap. 'Have fuuun.' He flashed him a grin.

'I bet you think you're so clever right now.' Liam narrowed his green eyes.

James chuckled, grabbing his jacket and car keys. He waved his hand behind him as he headed for the door, calling out softly, 'See you later, poopy duty.'

As he closed the door behind him, James heard Liam sigh-growl and Chad click his tongue. James smiled fondly – he enjoyed living with them all, they were family to him, they were his pack.

He got into his sleek, dark grey electric car he'd just had cleaned, and drove off – he was the model of a ruggedly handsome rich man, the very image of a Sharpe Alpha.

When James arrived at the grocery store, he strode along the aisles, getting all the items he needed for the household of seven. He clocked a couple of guys following and eyeing him suspiciously. He ignored them but remained alert. Something about their demeanour made him uneasy.

When James exited the store, as he placed the items in the trunk of the car, he noticed more men coming from an alley behind the store. This wasn't normal.

James closed the trunk and immediately put out his elbows in a parry as two men tried to punch him from behind. He shoved them off him, turning to face his attackers, only for more of them to pounce on him and grab him from all sides before he could even grab his pistol.

He did not recognise his assailants, and if he used his powers in broad daylight, it would draw unwanted attention.

The group of men lifted James by the legs and upper arms, and carried him into the alley. James kicked one of them off him but another took that one's place, holding James with a strength that prevented James from moving. They pinned him to the ground and one of them removed James's gun from its holster, giving James no choice but to defend himself the way he knew how.

Hands still free, James reached out towards his assailants. Careful not to extend his claws, he grabbed the two men who held his arms, gripping their collars, and pulled inwards, slamming their heads together – he used his brute strength without giving any hint that he had superpowers. Still, with this many men attacking him, it was tempting to draw on his special abilities.

He used more of his might to break free completely before the men pounced on him again, pushing him down as one of them landed a kick on James's spine, sending the Sub-Alpha sprawling to the gravel. Bracing himself with his hands, James fell onto his stomach and the men got on top of him, pinning him completely.

James could no longer move, not unless he used his werewolf abilities, and he was yet uncertain who his attackers were.

'James Sharpe,' one of them sneered, his voice deep and fearsome. 'I'd be careful if I were you.' The man walked with heavy boots and came to stand before James. He crouched, taking James's chin between his fingers and squeezing. He forced James's face to tilt up to meet his gaze.

The man wore army boots, denim pants that were sleeker than the average brand, and a designer leather jacket. There were tattoos on the backs of his hands with a symbol James did not recognise, though it was hard to see them properly from this angle. His stubble was long and unruly, while his hair bore a close shave with a pattern that looked similar to the symbol tattooed on each of his hands. He appeared to be in his mid-thirties, like James. And a menacing glare reflected in his blue-grey eyes.

'Who the hell are you?' James growled.

The imposing man grinned sinisterly. 'Who, indeed?' He came closer and whispered into James's ear. 'A word of advice, James Sharpe: no one likes a weak Alpha.'

James let out a guttural sigh – he was being attacked by his own kind.

'And *we* don't like your new allies,' the man went on. 'So before you bring ruin to all our kind, I suggest you change course. Ensure you are *not* the one named as the new Alpha . . .' He paused. This demand did not surprise James one bit. '. . . Or ditch the vampire.' *That* enraged James.

Roaring, James extended his claws, allowing his teeth to sharpen, and with all his strength pushed against the werewolves pinning him. They, in turn, extended claws, growling in response. James jumped to his feet and swiped at the tattooed man before him.

This one blocked James's arm and pushed him into one of his lackeys. The others moved to his signals and gave him room to fight James on his own terms. This man was an Alpha, James concluded.

The Alpha's eyes glowed as they flared yellow and he leapt at James with great speed. James ducked, reaching up with speed as the man passed above him – James retrieved his gun from his attacker as the man landed behind him instead. James spun and kicked the back of his opponent's legs, sending him to the ground. He grabbed the man's neck, claws digging into his it. The man pushed his arms out and shoved James off him.

James was on top of him again, this time pulling back the safety of his pistol as he landed on the other Alpha. At the same time as the Alpha's werewolves trained their guns on James, James pressed the muzzle of his gun directly under his enemy's chin, pushing against his throat.

Everyone froze.

'Shoot me and you're dead,' the Alpha growled, eyes darting to his pack and back.

'Then we're at a standstill,' James clapped back, his voice rough. If any of them dared shoot James, their Alpha would also be dead.

No one dared make the next move.

'Who are you?' James demanded. 'You're an Alpha. Where from?'

'We're your opposition to the alliance your pack has made with the vampires,' sneered the man. 'You disgrace us with that boyfriend of yours.'

'Husband,' corrected James.

'Werewolves and vampires don't mix.' The man paused. He suppressed a smirk before narrowing his eyes with a new scowl. 'Go ahead then, kill me. You have witnesses that you'd be betraying your kind.'

'You're the one who attacked *me*,' countered James.

'We're protecting our people from the likes of you who will bring ruin to all werewolves.'

'So you don't like the idea of the alliance.' James pressed harder with his gun. He knew he was being allowed to question this Alpha, but his senses remained alert in case someone decided to be brave and pounce on him from behind.

'Other packs have already agreed to this alliance and have begun making reparations with the vampires of their cities and towns to make amends and to rebuild the bridges that were burnt centuries ago,' James went on.

'We're here to ensure it all fails, and that werewolves and vampires see that there cannot be any alliance between our kinds,' the other Alpha snapped back. 'We're going to bring back the glory of the werewolf kind and dominate all beings of the Underworld.'

James snorted, opening his mouth to retort when a group of security officers came running into the alley.

The Alpha shoved a startled James off him and the group of werewolves ran the other way, leaving James alone with the security detail.

'Sir?'

James spun to face them, pointing behind him with his gun. 'Can you believe, they jumped me!'

'Yes, an eyewitness reported a man of your description being taken into the alley by numerous other men.' The other officers hurried after the werewolves who were now out of view.

'Took you long enough to get here, though,' James noted with annoyance.

'There was . . . an altercation between some folks near the entrance of the store,' the officer explained.

Of course – the other members of the pack, there to cause a distraction while those accompanying the Alpha pounced on James.

Sighing, James shook his head. 'It's fine. It was just a random scuffle. I doubt these men'll come back to your store.' James showed the man his ID.

The officer's posture changed – he obviously recognised the name – and he nodded. 'Of course, Mister Sharpe.' To humans, the Sharpes were a mafia who owned many businesses – no one wanted to ruffle their feathers. 'If you need anything . . .' He trailed off.

James nodded and waved the officer off as he returned to his car. He leaned back in the driver's seat.

'What just happened?' he breathed to himself before powering the car and shifting gears.

* * *

James slammed the door open, stomping into the house.

'Shoes, James. Shoes!' complained Rachel, who was sitting in the living room with the others, breast-feeding the baby.

James's face was one of anger and shock, and Chad clocked how his heart was beating abnormally fast for someone who had just gone grocery shopping.

Rachel, for her part, recognised something was wrong too and her expression changed. 'What happened?'

'I got jumped,' declared James.

Chad's heart began to race and his body tensed. He immediately stood and walked over to James, wanting only to protect him. 'What? By whom?'

'Another rival mafia?' Liam asked cautiously.

'Another Alpha.'

Rachel stood. 'I'll let you boys talk in private.' She left the room, rocking Hikaru in her arms.

'A pack of werewolves?! Do you know who?' asked Chad.

James shook his head. 'I got no names out of him. But they are a group of werewolves who are opposed to the vampire-werewolf alliance and want to make werewolves the dominant beings of the Underworld, from what I understood.'

'That's not good,' voiced Julian, leaning forward in his seat. 'Not if they're attacking you, and in broad daylight.'

Chad remembered the Gregorian chanting he'd heard the other day. '*Tenebrārum inferos dominabimur.*' he muttered. 'We shall rule the Underworld.'

'That mean something?' asked James.

'It's something I overheard the other night but didn't think much of it,' explained Chad. James scowled and Chad met his gaze with a grim expression. 'Back when vampires and werewolves attempted to band together the first time, the leader of the group opposing such an alliance was a vampire. She . . .' Chad closed his eyes and sighed. 'She seduced me and I loved her.'

'Seduced you!' exclaimed Liam.

Chad's voice trembled as he replied. 'She seduced me. And then she . . . broke me.' He squeezed his eyes tighter. 'Never have I questioned my own reality or sanity more than when I was with her.'

James put a hand on Chad's shoulder and squeezed. James had heard the story before, of how this vampire had broken Chad, minus a few details. Chad knew James felt his pain.

He opened his eyes, feeling saddened by the memory. 'She gave me vital information that I used to help the vampires fight those under her command.'

'You betrayed her?' asked Julian.

'No.' Chad turned to face his friend, though his eyes unfocused as he ruefully recalled that time in his life. 'She gave me a choice. She knew I would either use the infor-mation to help her or go against her. When we parted ways, after a long and tormented kiss, as I leaned forward, watching her walk away, my heart pained, I knew I would use the information to go against her.'

Chad bowed his head. 'She disappeared after that, never to be seen again. Though now, with such a group making its intentions known, despite the leader of this immediate group being a werewolf Alpha, I wonder if she is the one leading a larger group opposing our alliance.'

The men grew silent.

Liam put a hand to his chin, thinking. 'There have been groups on both sides – vampires and werewolves alike – who were reluctant or even opposed to the alliance and have not agreed to accept an alliance yet, but none have expressed any hint of wanting to reignite any wars between vampires and werewolves. They've wanted nothing to do with either and have asked to be left alone.'

'I don't know who these werewolves are,' repeated James. 'I've never seen them before.'

Chad placed his hands on James's arms – his husband was vibrating with anger. 'You're shaken.' He was worried too. 'They attacked *you*.'

James stared at the floor. 'If I become the Alpha, because I'm married to you, Chad, it would be a statement to vampires and werewolves alike. Our relationship, out in the open as it is, with this alliance between your coven and my pack, is unprecedented.' James swallowed. 'I was given a warning. I think if I don't heed it, they'll come after me again.'

Dread filled Chad's heart. 'What was the warning?'

'I either not become Alpha or I . . .' James's eyes finally met Chad's with a fiery gaze and Chad knew right away. He felt a pang in his gut. James cupped Chad's cheeks with his hands. 'Chad, baby, I'm fine.'

'Your heart rate and face tell me otherwise.'

James's eyes softened and he leaned his forehead on Chad's. 'Don't worry about it. We'll find out more next time they try to jump me.'

Chad backed away, shocked by the statement. 'You mean you *want* them to jump you?'

James scowled. 'I want to learn who they are, where they're from, who else is with them. I want to know who my enemies are.'

Julian and Liam stood.

'James,' said Julian, 'if you fight other werewolves, won't that make you an outcast?'

'I will protect our alliance,' asserted James. 'My pack accepted Chad immediately after seeing what you were all willing to do to protect us. I was ready to walk away and leave them, but they accepted that it was time for werewolves and vampires to band together. They accepted that my love for this one vampire was that strong and forgave that I'd been willing to leave. They recognised our passion, and knew it was possible for there to be true peace, reconciliation, friendship, and love between vampires and werewolves. Other packs will accept the alliance too. If I fight those who oppose it . . .' He sighed gutturally.

'They believe in the old ways,' concluded Chad. He frowned, thinking. 'There must be vampires who speak of the old ways too, traditionalists.'

'Traditionalists? That might explain why I was jumped only by men.' James put a hand to his head. 'Enough analysing. This is getting us nowhere. I need to get ready for tonight, and groceries need bringing in from the car.'

James turned, leaving Chad with an uneasy feeling about the situation. He was unsure what exactly was the cause of the unease, but something about it didn't sit right with him.

* * *

James had his duffle bag ready, but he hesitated by the door. He was reluctant to leave.

'Baby,' Chad said gently, walking over to him. His eyes told him he felt the same way James did.

So far, James had always gone alone when Feral Night arose. At the beginning, he had been self-conscious about Chad seeing him feral, but only because his exes had not enjoyed that or had been weird about it. James wanted nothing more than for Chad to discover all of him – they were married! They were lovers and newlyweds.

Their union, his and Chad's, was so unusual, James always chickened out. James was afraid Chad did not want to see him feral, so he never voiced his desire, to avoid the answer that would sadden and disappoint him. Instead, he always hinted, hoping Chad might offer to tag along. Despite that, with every full moon, he could feel it more and more, ready to finally shed his hesitancy and show all of himself to his husband.

'I hate to leave you for a full night,' admitted James.

'I know.' Chad wrapped his arms around James. 'You say that every time.'

'I feel like I'm going off . . . cheating or something,' James sighed.

Chad chuckled. 'You are going off, but I know it's because it's Feral Night.' Chad's fingers caressed the back of James's neck, sending a sweet tingle down his spine – Feral Night always increased arousal. Chad tenderly played with James's hair. 'I trust you and I know you'd never cheat on me, James.'

James felt a pang of yearning. It had been three months and three weeks since they married, having been together more than a year – James felt he should be able to ask him, but he just could not. Fear of rejection, he surmised, was at play.

Every full moon, he'd drive off to the forest, do his thing with all the other werewolves, and leave Chad alone that night. James had to leave before sundown and could only return after sunrise. If he wanted Chad to tag along, they'd have to set the car up. It was a hassle he *wanted* to be obliged to take care of.

Chad kissed James sweetly, hands still playing with his hair. It was enough to make James *feel* feral. Deliberately pushing Chad against the wall, James growled in his throat, his lips never leaving his husband's.

'I wish I could take you right now,' James whispered, his voice husky. 'I wish there was time.'

Chad smiled tenderly. 'I'll see you later.'

James bit his lower lip. 'You bet.' He kissed Chad hungrily, opening his mouth to taste him fully before reluctantly pulling away.

Backing up, James sighed once more before leaving the house for the night. Again, he assumed Chad might feel weird seeing him feral, and James was unable to voice his desire to share that side of himself with Chad.

He drove down to his usual spot – already many other werewolves had parked their vehicles. James took his wedding ring off his finger and kissed it. The fading light reflected on the white gold as James placed it in the centre console storage compartment. He stripped down and stepped out into the cool spring night.

He was on edge. Being attacked by another werewolf – one he did not know, one who was not part of the new alliance – made his hair stand on end, but he quelled the emotions. This was not the night to dwell on that, it was time to be free.

James's muscles twitched as the last light descended on the horizon. His skin itched as his hair began to grow into long fur all over his body and his large muscles jerked again as he howled into the night.

Roaring savagely, James leapt forward and landed on all fours, and bayed into the dense forest where his packmates were already roaming free. He enjoyed the wind in his fur. This was the only time – every moon – where he could feel these sensations. It was liberating and exhilarating.

A blur caught James's attention and he turned to it, standing on his hind legs. He bared his teeth, growling ferociously at the intruder. He could smell a vampire.

'It's okay, it's me.'

James refocused as the blur stopped before him and he breathed in the familiar scent. A surprised welp escaped him and he backed away reflexively. Before him stood his husband, his glowing eyes already dimming back to their usual charcoal.

James was shocked, but given the circumstances, he could not voice it in words.

As if Chad knew, he reached his hand out to caress James's snout. 'It's okay. I'm sorry I surprised you, I . . . wanted to find you.' His eyes softened. 'I wanted to see you, needed to be in your presence and make sure you were safe.'

James let out a throaty sigh of appreciation, tender longing tugging at his heart. He still had questions, yet his husband knew him so damn well, Chad answered knowing the question James could not voice.

'I knew it was you – I could smell you before I found you. You're my husband, I'd recognise you anywhere.'

Chad's eyes roamed the feral body before him. 'You're beautiful.' He smiled. 'I love you, James.'

Chad passed his hand along James's brown mane, stroking slowly, from his face all the way down his body. James closed his eyes, breathing deeply – oh, how he wished he could make love to his husband right now! The gesture was as electrifying as it was soothing, and his heart filled with delight.

James rubbed his snout on Chad and before he knew what he was doing, he pushed him onto the ground, pouncing on him.

Chad landed on his back – his eyes flared white and his canines extended. 'Oh, is that how you want to play this, eh?' He chuckled.

James licked Chad's face in answer and Chad laughed. He loved him so much. Even when James thought Chad did not want to see him thus, Chad found him to show him he need not hide any part of himself from him, for their love was greater than any inhibition. And right now, the only way James could show his affection and desire was with feral actions.

'I'll race you,' Chad challenged him.

James breathed gutturally in response, moving off Chad, and the two darted about throughout the forest and the night, roaring, laughing, and playfully licking and shoving.

Then, the sky gave the first hint of the approaching dawn. Chad stopped, panting, and turned to James. 'I must go.' James whimpered sadly. 'I'll see you soon, yeah.'

Chad kissed the side of James's feral face, stroking his fur. James wished he could shout *Wait!* But instead, he watched his husband back away from him and dash off with vampiric speed, leaving James feeling a sweet pang in his heart.

James stood tall on his hind legs, veins bulging and fur swaying on his large thighs, and turned his snout towards the sky. He roared with the power that coursed through him and howled one final time, and his packmates echoed a howling chorus.

As the sun rose, the fur on James's body began to recede back beneath his skin, and his muscles twitched until he was walking like a human again, the cool spring wind tickling his naked skin.

He hurried back to his car and dressed. He paused to stare fondly at his ring before putting it on, and sped home to find Chad waiting for him in the corridor, arms crossed and smiling as he leaned against the wall, keeping his distance from the door so the sun would not reach him.

James rushed to him and, as Chad wrapped his arms around him, kissed him deeply, his tongue finding Chad's and tasting the vampire's recent feed. He pulled away, breathless, leaning one arm on the wall above Chad's head and placing the other on his face.

'I'm sorry I surprised you,' Chad began.

'Don't be. It's not that I'm ashamed of that form, it's just . . . I never thought you'd want to see it. I always lost my nerve whenever I wanted to ask you to come with me.'

'I love all of you, James, of course I'd want to share in that part of you with you. We're married now and every Feral Night I ache for you, just to be with you and witness the beauty that you are in that form.' Chad's eyes flared, making James's stomach flutter. 'You are magnificent, James Sharpe. I love you so much.'

'Oh, Chad, baby.' James smiled. 'Thank you for finding me and taking the initiative. You have no idea the joy it brought me.' He brought his mouth to Chad's ear and whispered. 'I'm not done being feral.'

Chad breathed in sharply, squeezing James's back and pressing his cheek to his, making James's desire mount. James pressed himself against Chad, letting him feel how ready he was for him, how ready he was to fully taste him.

The door to the master bedroom opened and out walked Rachel and Keisuke.

'Good to see you both up!' Keisuke greeted them with a half-yawn. He was buttoning his shirt, dressing for work, though his shoulder-length black hair was a bit tangled at the back 'We're running a bit late, think you could tend to the baby?'

James sighed, hanging his head as Chad chuckled, shaking his head. 'We'll continue this later,' James promised.

'I'll hold you to that.'

Chapter Two

The sky turned from pink to indigo as the sun disappeared behind the horizon.

'All right,' Chad called out, motioning for his friends to follow him. He stepped out into the cool night, breathing in the fresh scent of spring. 'Liam, with me. Julian, James' – Chad pointed – 'stand there.'

James and Julian exchange a puzzled glance, stepping aside as Chad had instructed and standing on the sidelines. They folded their arms, both a near mirror of each other's stance.

Liam waited for Chad to continue, his gaze expectant. 'What's this about?'

'You might have exceptional instincts, but you still need to train,' reminded Chad.

'We've been training for a year!' complained Liam. 'I think I'm good.'

'With the dagger, I mean, we have not.' Chad inclined his head. 'And a vampire never stops training. You think I haven't survived all these millennia without continued training?'

Liam hesitated. 'What if I accidentally graze you?'

'I'm not worried. Besides,' Chad smirked, 'you're a *Sui Generis Lamia,* if you accidentally graze me, I'm sure you'll kiss it all better.'

'Oi!' Julian warned angrily. 'My husband's not kissing anyone but me.'

Chad laughed. 'Will you relax, I'm just teasing.'

Julian turned to James, pointing a thumb in Chad's direction. 'How do you put up with this?'

James shrugged. 'I'm not jealous, I guess.' Julian snorted. Yeah, Chad knew as much as everyone else did that wasn't true.

Liam took the sleek slim dagger from its sheath and waved it about, taking a defensive stance. Chad placed a hand on his back and an arm out diagonally in front of him, palm open, fingers close.

'Come at me.'

Liam lunged forward and swiped with the dagger. Bringing his arm up, Chad blocked with ease, using a variety of techniques he'd learnt throughout his lifetime, and within seconds, he had disarmed Liam and taken the dagger from him.

Liam stopped and gaped at Chad. 'Well, that's me being proven a total noob.'

Chad laughed, amused. 'Your teacher is the oldest vampire alive.' Chad thought about that for a moment. 'One of them.' That was technically true.

'Yeah, who else is as old as you, huh?' Liam grinned as Chad handed him back his dagger, never letting go of the hilt. 'Speaking of which, you must know the answer to this enigma, ancient as you are, because I still can't wrap my head around how supernatural beings can sustain fire, but us vamps can't sustain the sun. Why is that, is it the rays?'

'You know, I've been trying to answer that one for millennia. We can stand in fire of any heat and walk out unscathed. I mean, your hair will get singed but that's about it. But the sun . . . we just melt – and only us vamps.'

Liam pointed with his free hand at the others. 'I bet it's the U.V. rays. Those things are dangerous, even to humans.'

Chad chuckled then shook his head, refocusing. 'We try again. This time, anticipate my movements.' Chad backed away and resumed his former stance.

Liam positioned himself again and came at Chad with vampiric speed. Chad swiped his arm away, batting Liam's other arm with his hand, but this time Liam dodged and kicked Chad in the stomach. Liam pounced on Chad, sending him careening to the ground, the knife gleaming above his face as he landed on top of him.

Going from a wide to narrow stretch, he brought his legs in, pinning Chad onto his back, with the elder vampire's arms stuck between Liam's knees.

Chad nodded. 'Okay, that was impressive.'

'All right, all right,' chided James, 'straddle your *own* husband.'

Liam stood, taking a step back, and helped Chad to his feet as the four men chuckled.

'Now, how serious was that joke, really?' Chad asked, curiosity tugging at him. He gave James a sly smile and James feigned surprise.

Someone's phone vibrated. 'It's my aunt,' announced James, glancing at the screen. He answered and put the phone on speaker.

'James, come immediately to the stadium,' came Adrienne's authoritative voice. 'It's urgent.'

'O-kay?' James hesitated. 'Is everything all right?'

'Absolutely! Just hurry up and get here. Bring Chad. Oh, and your roommates can come too.'

'You mean you want the *Sui Generis Lamia* present,' James concluded.

'Yes, but his husband can attend as well – they're after all extended pack members by proxy.' There was laughter in her voice. 'See you all soon.' She hung up and James sighed loudly.

'When I'm made Alpha,' he began, 'this is something I'm *not* going to do.'

'Let's go find out what your aunt wants with us,' said Chad, placing his hand on his husband's shoulder.

James smiled and took Chad's hand in his, interlacing their fingers. His large hand was warm, and it brought comfort to Chad, for everywhere there were reminders of what it had taken to create their alliance, not to mention that the circumstances of meeting and falling in love with James saddened Chad even while he did his best to remain distracted.

* * *

James, Chad, Liam and Julian strode into the stadium – a large field, perfect for sports games and owned by the Sharpes. Bright lights lit up the field and James quickly became aware that the seats were packed.

As soon as the four of them walked onto the field where Adrienne and Martin stood, a ruckus of roars and cheers erupted from the onlooking pack members. James's heart nearly stopped in his chest, skipping a beat, as he realised what this was.

Chad beside him caught on too. 'When you're made Alpha . . .' he muttered.

James opened up his arms. 'Aunt Adrienne, what's this?'

Adrienne, tall and imposing, her long dark hair cascading down her voluptuous and muscular body, smiled fondly at James.

'It's time,' she declared. 'And thus I've called the entire pack to be present – all the families that comprise our pack are in attendance. All who could be here are here.'

James knew of a few, especially one friend in particular, who were either travelling or had other circumstances keeping them away from this occasion. That Adrienne had been able to gather this many from the pack was impressive.

'And since this ceremony requires your partner to be present,' Adrienne went on, 'well, we couldn't do this during the day, could we?'

James continued to stare at her in disbelief as he came to stand before her. The others beamed at him.

'It is time for the induction!' Martin called out into a mic. The crowd grew quiet. Martin turned to his wife, presenting the microphone to her.

Adrienne took the mic and began her speech. 'Werewolves of the Sharpe pack, friends and allies, I have called you here tonight because it is time for me to step down and retire as the pack's Alpha, and to leave this pack in the capable hands of a new Alpha.'

James's heart hammered with anticipation. It was sinking in now, this dream of his was a reality, and Chad was right here beside him, holding his hand tightly and grinning madly.

'More and more vampires and werewolves are voicing their support,' reported Adrienne to the crowd, 'for the success of this alliance – an alliance that was started by my nephew James Sharpe and the vampires with whom he associates.'

Adrienne motioned the three vampires and the pack members cheered them. 'They took initiative, they helped werewolves, they saved our lives, and they were the first to set aside old grievances for the sake of the future of all beings of the Underworld. They treated each of us as one of them, and through that, I learnt that their values are not so different from ours. In kindred, they are as one of us.'

Adrienne winked at Liam, who smiled and winked back at her, as though they were sharing an inside joke.

'The people of the Underworld want change,' Adrienne went on, looking up at the spectators, 'they want – to use Keisuke's words – an evolution, not a revolution. They are ready to *make* amends and to *accept* amends, not retribution.

'Seeing as our pack,' she turned to James, 'and your husband's coven were the first to sign this treaty, other werewolves want to see us make a statement in the face of those who oppose our reconciliation with the vampires. Both peoples want to see a strong front. Thus, I have decided to expedite my retirement as the pack's Alpha.'

James's stomach was doing backflips and somersaults. He was bursting to roar, but he waited for his cue.

'With your union, especially since it is fresh,' continued Adrienne, 'it tells the whole of the Underworld and the Upper Realms how serious we are in this prospective future.' Her voice grew heavy with emotion, fond emotion. 'James, the pack has spoken, they've accepted you as the new Alpha and Chad as your Partner-Alpha.'

James could feel her pride for him and it nearly moved him to tears.

Adrienne nodded to James and handed him the mic. 'Sharpe pack,' he shouted. 'I am James Sharpe, contender for the title of Alpha. Many have vied for this title, all of whom have been worthy rivals. A pack's Alpha protects his pack, and ensures the pack thrives. An Alpha knows what to sacrifice and when to compromise. And an Alpha knows when not to back down and instead hold his ground.'

James glanced at his friends, whose smiles encouraged him. 'For years I have not let anyone stand in my way to get to this day, and I won't let anyone stand in my way now either. Anyone threatens my pack, and

I will strike them down. Anyone endangers any pack member, and they will taste my fist. For I, James Sharpe, will prove to you how strong I am as your Alpha!'

Werewolves roared, banging their feet on the floor and clapping enthusiastically.

Adrienne turned to Chad, tilting her chin up at him. She took the mic from James. 'Chad, you are the very first vampire in all our kinds' history to be accepted as Partner-Alpha and to have this honour. I understand you will continue to act as an elder to your coven.' She inclined her head forward. 'We will expect you to do your duty for the pack, but will respect that you will not compromise your duty as one of the most ancient vampires to walk this earth.'

Chad bowed regally. 'It truly is an honour, Milady Adrienne.' He straightened.

'Adopting formal language?' chuckled James. Chad winked at him before he grew serious once more.

Chad knelt on one knee, head bowed, then he met Adrienne's gaze with intensity. She held the mic so his voice could be heard by all. 'I promise – no, I *vow* – that I will do my due as the Partner-Alpha. I shall not put my own desires ahead of the needs of the pack or of the alliance we have forged together.' Chad's eyes flared and his canines extended, and he shouted with conviction, 'This is my oath to the pack as the husband of James Sharpe.'

The crowd whooped, shouting out, 'Chad Sharpe! Chad Sharpe! Chad Sharpe!'

Chad blushed significantly, suppressing a laugh. 'Now who told them I took your name when we married?' he muttered under his breath. He rose, and looked up at the werewolves gathered, and all grew silent once more.

James stood tall, calling out. 'I promise to lead the pack with honour and glory, as you have, Aunt Adrienne.' He looked from Chad to the people – to his pack. 'I too vow to honour the pack, and I promise to continually prove myself worthy of this title as the leader of all those who now fall under my protection.' James grinned. He ripped his shirt open, tossing the two halves to the ground and roaring thunderously with all his werewolf might, mustering a deep reverberation within him.

The crowd roared loudly in response. Julian and Liam whistled, and shouted out, 'Yeah!'

'There is one tradition left before I can truly accept this title, however.' James turned to Adrienne.

'Oh, you are so going down, my dear nephew. I hope you won't disappoint your parents too much.' Adrienne rolled up her sleeves and removed her heels.

James laughed. 'That's what you think, Aunt Adrienne. I've been training with vampires. Let's see what you've got against that, hah!'

Everyone cheered and shouted out as James and Adrienne squared off against each other. They both lunged forward, claws extended and teeth bared, pupils slightly narrowing vertically as they exuded their werewolf abilities. Roaring, James spun, bringing his aunt down onto her back. She rolled away quickly and bounced up, somersaulting around James and sending him a kick in the face.

'Oooh!' went the pack members.

James chuckled as he flipped backwards, landing several paces away. Adrienne came at him again and they locked arms, pushing against the other. Her strength was second to none, James knew. It was her secret weapon. But he was larger, thus his resistance won out. Eventually, Adrienne staggered back and James pinned her down once more. Adrienne lifted her arms in surrender.

'I wouldn't want to embarrass you with a comeback,' Adrienne teased. She smirked. 'My Alpha.'

James laughed, helping his aunt up.

Martin shouted into the mic. 'Let today be known as the day when my wife stepped down as Alpha and James Sharpe took the mantle. May his reign as Alpha bring glory to the pack!' Tumultuous applause and raucous cheers rose up from the gathered pack members.

James, Martin, and Adrienne roared at the crowd gathered. James pulled his aunt to him by the arm and hugged her.

'Thank you for granting me this honour, Aunt Adrienne.' James allowed himself to shed a tear as he laughed his joy.

'Thank you for ushering in a new era for all werewolves. The honour is mine to see you take the mantle.' She pulled away and placed her hands on his face. 'I am so proud of you!'

James saw his parents and other Sharpe family members run down from their seats to come give him bear hugs. Chad, Liam, and Julian were among the group hugging James, congratulating him, and together they lifted James onto their shoulders. Many called for Chad to be lifted with James. Before James knew it, he and Chad were floating above the crowd.

The werewolves carried James and Chad around the stadium, all while cheering out, 'James Sharpe!' and 'Chad Sharpe!' At times, shouting their titles of Alpha and Partner-Alpha with their names.

James beamed at Chad, whose eyes twinkled at him. He reached for his hand. James's heart was bursting – his dream had come true, he was finally the Alpha. He leaned towards his husband from over his pack members' shoulders and kissed him hungrily, breathlessly opening his mouth and lacing his tongue with his husband's. Cheers and whoops encouraged him to continue.

Party poppers sounded off and James spotted Victoria prancing about, offering jello shots to everyone.

'When did *she* get here!' laughed James.

And then music boomed from the speakers as the party truly started.

* * *

There were still a couple of hours before morning would dawn – the party had raged on all night. James, Chad, Liam, and Julian walked home, the two vampire husbands drunker than Chad had ever seen them.

'How does it feel to be the Alpha?' asked Liam, swaying as he walked ahead.

James's reply was a loud yawn. 'This Alpha needs his sleep.'

'You are sooo drunk, Liam,' Julian remarked.

'And you're not?' retorted Liam, his speech rapid if somewhat slurred.

'You get more emphatic when you're drunk,' remarked Julian.

'So what!'

Chad chuckled. 'Am I the only sober one?'

'You!' began James, a tad less drunk than the two vampires. He pointed at Chad, his finger close to his face. 'Are not sober.'

Chad had to agree, he did drink quite a lot, but he had stopped much earlier too.

The four of them staggered into the house. Liam clumsily stopped in the middle of the corridor near the door. Julian bumped into him, hugging him from behind and resting his head on his back. James bumped into Julian, and hugged them both.

'I love you so much, you two. You're the best house-mates a werewolf could have – the best vampire friends I could have asked for.'

The scene warmed Chad's heart. He felt the fire within him again, the oath he had made to the pack. He was a vampire, a vampire elder – the most ancient – loyal to his coven, and now also a Partner-Alpha to a werewolf pack. He had responsibilities to both peoples now, and to the alliance. If Chad wanted to be the Partner-Alpha the pack deserved, the husband and Partner-Alpha *James* deserved, he needed to sort through his emotions and get over this grief that haunted him.

Chad waited for James to be in bed before slipping out of the house – the Alpha had plopped onto the bed as soon as they entered their bedroom upstairs, having only stripped down to his underwear before, and had fallen asleep before Chad was done brushing his teeth.

The sky was clear and starlit, and Chad relished the cool May breeze that gently caressed his face.

He walked through the neighbourhood and into the next as he reached the avenue that led directly to the riverbank.

He stopped, sighing, feeling that familiar ache in his heart, the ache he wished to quell, the ache that made him feel guilty, as though he was betraying someone for hurting about that one loss.

In his peripheral vision, he noticed the corner shop he so often passed in front of when going and coming from the river. He realised that the lights inside weren't because it was a security measure but because it was open all night. He decided to enter. He wasn't sure what he wanted to buy – a snack, perhaps something to smoke, even if he wasn't a smoker – anything that could distract him from this sensation that tugged at his heart.

'Hello!' a friendly voice greeted him before a scrunched-up ball of paper whizzed past from one side of the shop into a garbage can that was placed at the other end. It went straight in. 'Haha! Take that!'

A young woman who looked no more than twenty years old walked to the cash register and leaned on the counter.

'Never seen *you* here before – you new in the neighbourhood?'

'Sort of.' Chad *was* still discovering parts of this end of town; this road was a bit removed from the house.

Chad stared at the girl. Her hair, sun-kissed with a balayage that made her amber eyes stand out, was long and wavy, and her little mannerisms reminded him of Mandy.

She lifted her brows. 'Are you just gonna stare at me all night?'

'I'm sorry,' Chad looked down at the counter, where some items being sold were held behind a locked slider. 'You remind me of someone I knew.' He looked up at the young woman again and felt the sadness that came with thinking of Mandy and everything she had taken away from him. And yet, her actions had led to all this – the alliance, James – in a way.

'Judging by the look on your face, it doesn't sound like a good thing.'

'Oh . . . well . . . she died.'

'Oh, I'm so sorry.' The clerk's eyes softened. 'And here I was thinking you were just being a creep.'

Chad laughed self-consciously. 'No, she . . . was a close friend, like a sister.' He searched for his words. 'You have some cute mannerisms, that's all.'

The girl grinned and tilted her head. 'You flirting with me? I mean, you're all right for a guy who looks like he could be twice my age. I mean, I'm not *opposed*—'

'I'm married!' Chad lifted his left hand, palm inward, and showed her the gleaming band around his finger.

'Wow, is that silver?'

'White gold . . . with palladium.'

'Neat. Check this out.' The girl pulled out a large coin of silver from her wallet. 'Just ordered these. Exclusive mint. Pure silver.' She held it closer to Chad's face and he leaned back.

'Very nice,' he admitted, taking a subtle but cautious step back.

'I ordered a bunch of these babies. My roommate, Evan, keeps going on about how *digital* investments are the way of the future, but I say, if I can't hold it, what's the point?' She tucked the coin back into her wallet and patted her pocket. 'Anyway, you here to buy something?'

'Yeah, maybe some chocolate or something.'

The young woman pointed at a shelf that displayed many choices. She passed him one. 'Go place that on one of those higher shelves over there – anywhere.'

Chad hesitated. 'Why?'

'Because! I'm bored and now I've got company. I want to show off my skills.'

Shaking his head and suppressing a laugh, Chad placed the chocolate bar on a tall shelf at the other end of the shop. The young woman took a scrunched ball of paper and tossed it at the chocolate bar from behind the counter. The ball of paper hit the chocolate, knocking it off the shelf, and it fell into Chad's hands.

'Yes! Perfect score, every time. My aim is *on fleek.*'

Chad chuckled, shaking his head again. 'Not bad.' He walked back to the counter and placed the chocolate bar on it. 'How much do I owe you?'

'On the house, for letting me entertain you. It's cool.'

'Okay.' Chad continued to stare at her, even after he took the wrapped confection. 'I was wrong. You might have some similar traits to my friend, but you're not like her.' He smiled.

'I'm not entirely sure how to react to that,' she admitted.

'My friend, she . . . betrayed me . . . and then she died.'

'Oohhh, gotcha. Well, enjoy your chocolate, wherever you're off to.'

'I'm going for a walk by the river,' said Chad. He didn't know why, but he felt he could tell her. Funny how things worked out sometimes – he couldn't tell his husband about his nighttime escapades by the river, but he could talk about Mandy to a complete stranger.

'Well then, enjoy your walk by the river.'

'Thanks.' Chad backed away, chocolate in hand, and left the shop.

Chad waited to be standing at his usual spot on the edge of the river to eat his snack. It had that strange aroma of way too many artificial ingredients tainting the flavour of chocolate that should taste more pure. Yet, Chad couldn't deny the sweetness of it actually made him forget his aching heart for a few minutes as he slowly chewed it.

He studied the wrapper, pausing to think back to the girl at the shop. He couldn't believe how much that girl reminded him of Mandy. She didn't look anything like her, and yet . . . she was so much like her even while she was not. She was carefree, confident, assertive, playful. She was beautiful and woman-like, yet young enough to retain an endearing child-like behaviour. Just like Mandy.

'No!' Chad said to himself. He would not think about that. If he closed his eyes, he could see Zack tormented on the ground, Zanitha's head blown off. *Whatevs!* Chad shut his eyes more tightly, a pain in his chest like none other he had ever felt. Why did this hurt so much?

He balled his hands into fists. That expression, that chuckle of hers. He wished he'd never heard it, he wished it hadn't been her who'd betrayed the coven.

Chad dashed back home with vampiric speed and hurried into the bedroom where James lay sprawled, arms stretched out, taking up all the space on their King-sized bed.

Chad needed to forget his ache and his guilt. Hence, he would make love to his husband – a desperate need to be distracted by the one person who knew how to make him feel good when he felt so dreer.

He pulled the covers off James, who grunted in his sleep, his large pecs rising and falling as he breathed. He tugged off James's boxers and relished the view of his husband's dangling penis.

Chad quickly undressed and climbed up on the bed over James, kissing his lips tenderly before gently trailing his canines along James's perfectly toned muscles all the way down, grazing his glowing, tawny skin.

James moaned, bending his leg, and a hand came to rest on Chad's head, caressing it and playing with his hair. Chad licked his way down the rest of the way, tracing the curve of James's pubis where his dick elongated to a fully erect length, and a groan escaped James's lips.

'Oh, Chad, baby.'

Enticed by the huskiness in his husband's voice, Chad licked down the other man's length. He spat on his thumbs and began stroking circles on James's shaft, while doing the same on his perineum with his other thumb.

'Oh, baby, yes.'

James's hand stroked Chad's head more tightly, grabbing onto his curly hair.

Chad continued his thumbing as he licked James's balls with vigour. James had perfect pubes on perfect testicles, and it turned Chad on, spurring him to keep licking.

'Fuck, Chad, stop teasing me. Just take me.' His voice was more growl than whimper.

Chad began sliding up and down, aroused by how much James was enjoying his sensual taunts. Chad's tongue came to jab at James's smooth tip – James growled, his nails extending. The werewolf's hands pounded the bed. He grappled the sheets and dug his nails into the mattress as Chad took him in his mouth. It was enough to make Chad forget how he felt.

Chad sucked hard on his lover's cock as the werewolf suppressed a growl that would have been too loud, even in a room with thick walls. James began to buck his hips up and down as Chad sucked faster. Chad engulfed the Alpha's cock deeper, as though to swallow it whole – James let a closed-mouth shout out and Chad felt James squirt into the back of his throat, warm and creamy.

Chad swallowed, sucking more, and then swallowed again, continuing until there was nothing left to suck.

He slowly pulled his lips off James's still erect length as it slid out of his mouth. James was staring at him with lust in his eyes, his brown eyes flaring pale and yellow from his sharp werewolf instincts.

In one swift motion, James pulled Chad's face to his, and his mouth was devouring his lips, growls vibrating on Chad's lips. His stubble was longer and it prickled Chad's face. Chad rose, sliding upwards as James slapped his ass with his cock.

Chad could feel James still had more in him and could go another round. He lowered himself, kissing his way down to his husband's right nipple, and nibbled gently. He licked lower and up again, gliding the lapel of his tongue along the natural strokes of his husband's chest hair, and stopped at the nipple.

Chad felt the pulse of James's heart beneath his pectoral as Chad flicked his tongue over it. James's broad chest rose as he breathed elatedly, and Chad took the nipple between his teeth.

'Oh god,' James breathed out, his claws grazing Chad's back as his hands glided along it.

Chad wrapped his mouth around the nipple and he sucked it in his mouth, licking and nibbling it.

'Fuck, baby.'

Once again enticed by the moans James released, Chad took the other nipple between his thumb and index and began rubbing it between them.

'Fuck, Chad . . . baby.'

James's dick pulsed and twitched as he arched his back, and Chad felt it flick on his ass. He smiled as he continued to tantalise James.

James's arms spread out to grab hold of the bed again. 'Baby!' James cried out.

His cock flicked again, this time oozing more of his desire. Chad aligned himself with it, sliding down for it to meet his anus.

'Fuck me, baby,' James cried gruffly. 'Fuck my cock with your ass.'

James's cock slid right in, and Chad instantly felt a jolt of pleasure, his erection seeping precum onto James's stomach.

Chad slid up and down slowly, and he was already so close to succumbing to the ecstasy. James bucked as he came again, sending Chad into a dizzy frenzy, and the vampire surrendered to the sensations completely.

James grabbed hold of Chad's erection, pumping him hard. Chad plunged to kiss his husband – he shouted into James's mouth, the sound muffled. He held onto his man's shoulders tightly, feeling his eyes flare with vampiric instincts.

James's tongue danced across Chad's mouth, feeling the insides of his cheeks, dancing on his canines, and duelling his tongue. James repositioned himself to bring a hand behind Chad and he grabbed his ass, squeezing it before inserting a large finger into his rectum alongside his cock.

Chad jerked his head back, breaking away from James's mouth and biting his lip in order not to scream, as hot tingles pulsed in his pelvis. Sliding Chad's cock out of him, James pulled it up to his chest, letting it slide between his large pecs, and Chad could no longer contain himself.

He spilled all over James's pectorals, burying his face in his neck to stifle the scream that escaped his lips. His mouth met with James's again as the two kissed urgently while Chad's elation continued for a few more minutes, even after he was emptied.

Chad sighed loudly several times – whimpered spasms of his completing apex. Somehow James always knew how to elicit orgasms out of him with or without ejaculation.

Chad let himself collapse onto the bed and into James's strong embrace as the two fell into a deep sleep.

<h1 align="center">Chapter Three</h1>

As soon as James, Liam, and Julian entered the club, Victoria was on top of them, barking orders, her blond hair flawlessly coiffed as always and her nails sporting a fresh stiletto manicure, her nail polish as red as her lipstick.

'We've got a birthday party tonight – the rich kids,' she announced.

'Yeah, James filled us in,' said Liam.

'Liam, Julian, you're on bartending duty.' Victoria waggled a finger at them, her pointed nails awfully close to their faces. 'No vampiric speed. I know it's tempting but I need you two to behave.'

Liam and Julian shared a giggle. 'Did you hear that? She wants us to behave. No making out behind the bar,' Liam muttered to Julian.

'James,' Victoria turned to the Alpha, ignoring the two others' boyish chuckles, 'you're on the floor with me. We've got some private V.I.P. lounges to set up.'

'Yes, ma'am!'

Victoria dashed away.

'I can't believe her!' complained Liam, pointing his hand the way Victoria had gone, palm up. 'No vampiric speed, she says, and then she goes off . . . *with vampiric speed.*'

Julian chuckled. 'Let it go, Liam. She's the boss, she can do whatever she wants.'

'Oh, I'll show her about doing whatever she wants,' Liam grumbled as the two husbands made their way towards the bar.

Chuckling to himself, James prepared the lounges as ordered, with the proper arrangements as the clients had requested. He may be the Alpha now, but Victoria was the primary owner of the club between the two of them, and therefore the boss.

The club filled up fast with party-goers, most of whom were attendees to the rich kids' party. Though 'kids' wasn't so much what they were, if they were old enough to get drunk and go clubbing.

One of the groups from the private lounges had special orders. James brought the list to his friends.

'Special order from V.I.P. You think you can get to it quick?'

'Yes, sir!' said Liam.

'Oh, I like it when you call me sir,' James taunted playfully.

'Oi!' Julian warned.

'Didn't mean it like that.' Though James could understand Julian's glare, even if it was coupled with a smile. James *had* tried to hit it off with Liam before either of them knew the other was vampire and werewolf. As for Julian, well, James had witnessed his jealous streak firsthand.

James leaned forward against the bar, arms resting on it as he waited.

A young woman in a mini skirt and glittery top propped herself on one of the tall bar stools at the bar and ordered a drink from Liam.

'You are so cuuute!' she slurred, tucking her wavy hair behind her ear flirtatiously.

'Uh, thanks,' Liam hesitated, 'but I'm gay.'

'Oh my god, I'm sorry.' She covered her mouth.

'It's fine.' Liam flashed her a smile that was enough to make anyone melt, with those blond bangs of his and dazzling green eyes – and James had seen him with his canines extended. James remembered flirting with him back when he thought Liam was human, and if both were single today, James would probably be flirting with him now. He'd never admit it to Julian, though he had to Chad, but Liam was breathtakingly gorgeous.

Julian took one step and came to stand beside Liam, dark hair and blue eyes glowing under the club's flashing neons. 'And he's married' – he clasped Liam's hand and held it up – 'to me.'

'Aw, you two, and you're both so gorgeous.'

'Thanks. It's actually been a year now,' admitted Liam.

The young woman's eyes widened, and her voice reached a higher pitch. 'Aah! Congratulations! Oh my god, I'm so obsessed!' James chuckled at the way she was gushing.

'There was this guy who came into the corner shop where I work the other night – totally hot, but married. Like, why are all the hot guys in town either gay or married, or both? No offence, of course, but, like, am I just gonna stay single all my life, or what?!'

'You're still young,' noted James, turning towards her while still leaning on the bar counter. 'You've got years ahead of you to find the right man. And you're gorgeous too.'

'Oh my god, you're a bit older than I tend to go for, but like, are you single?'

James laughed. 'Sorry, I'm married.'

'Ah!' she shrilled, and James couldn't help but laugh. 'Lucky woman.' The girl sipped on her drink through the straw.

'Man, actually,' corrected James. 'I'm bi.'

The young woman sighed dramatically. 'But that guy the other night, let me tell you. As far as guys twice my age go . . .' She exhaled loudly, fanning herself. 'Tall, curly hair, driftwood-ish tone . . . And he had the shiniest of wedding bands too.' She squinted as she recalled. 'White gold, I think he said it was.'

'Oh?' all three men responded.

'Palla . . . laa . . . dium,' the young woman slurred.

James scowled, surprised and puzzled. 'Like this one?' He held up his hand, fingers relaxed to allow her to see his wedding band.

'Yeah! Exactly like it.' The girl nodded vigorously while sipping from her straw. Then her eyes widened. 'Wait, he's your husband, isn't he?'

'He is. May I ask when this was that you saw my husband?'

'Oh!' She turned on the bench to face James. 'It was like, 2:00 a.m. or something. He goes to the river at night, I think, he said.'

James frowned – he hadn't realised Chad snuck out of the house at night when James was asleep.

'Oh, crap, you didn't know, did you?' She made a face. 'Did I just drop him in it?'

'It's fine. I just . . .'

Julian placed the completed order of drinks on a tray for James just as another girl came and draped her arm around the young woman's.

'Dean's here,' she announced.

'Ugh. If Dean's here, then it's time to split.' She gave a small wave to the guys. 'Byeeeee!' And the two girls were off.

Feeling dismayed, James brought the tray of drinks to the V.I.P. lounge before he was told by another employee that someone in another private lounge was specifically asking for James Sharpe.

Taking a deep breath and refocusing on the task at hand, James entered the lounge – only to be hurled in by none other than the Alpha from the other day and shoved against the wall as his two goons shut the door behind them.

'Fuck!' cursed James.

'You and I never finished our little chat from the other day, James Sharpe,' the Alpha sneered.

'Get the fuck off me!' James shoved him away from him.

The Alpha's two bodyguards leapt towards James. James had his claws out and teeth pointed and bared in a flash as he hurled himself at the two men. He punched one in the gut, winding him and sending him to the ground. He kicked him in the chest and then swung his leg out to trip the other, punching him in the face and knocking him unconscious in the process.

As the other came at James anew, James unholstered his handgun and bashed the butt on the werewolf's head as he grabbed him, slamming him to the ground. Now both of the Alpha's bodyguards were lying unconscious.

Breathing heavily, James glared at the other Alpha, his gun held low but ready. 'What do you want?' he demanded. 'Let's speak Alpha to Alpha, you and me.'

'The message I want to convey is better expressed nonverbally.'

The Alpha lunged at James, grabbing him around the waist and pushing him to the wall. The force with which he shoved him was so intense, James nearly lost his grip on his gun. Winded, James kicked him off and aimed his weapon at his head. The other werewolf ducked and landed an uppercut to James's arm – again James nearly dropped his gun.

James spun him around as his assailant tried to take the pistol from him. He kicked the Alpha away and towards the wall. He lunged forward, sending his large fist towards his enemy's face.

At the last second, the other werewolf dodged and James punched the wall. He cursed as the Alpha got behind him. This one kicked James's gun hand and the pistol went skittering across the floor.

Kneeing James in the spine and pressing him against the wall as he bent James's arms back with one hand, the mystery Alpha brought his own gun up and pressed it beneath James's chin. James was in a deadlock.

He could feel the Alpha breathing on his neck. The man sneered. 'Now how does it feel to have your own tactic turn on you, hm?'

James pushed himself off the wall but the other Alpha, while his muscles were not as large as James's were, was stronger than him, and he pressed James harder against the wall – James glared at him as the side of his face was squashed against the wall.

The other Alpha pulled back the gun's safety. 'Let's try this again. I'm going to speak, and you're going to listen – and you're not going to try to fight back.'

James fumed gutturally.

'I hear there was an induction the other night.' He sneered sinisterly. 'You may have eliminated the Cromwells, but you'd better watch your back, James Sharpe. There's a new Alpha in town. And I'm not about to let the werewolf legacy plummet because of some weak Alpha who married a vampire.'

James seethed. He wanted to punch the man in the face. 'How dare you,' he growled.

'Of course, there's an easy solution to all this,' the mystery Alpha went on, his voice silvery.

'What do you want, then?' demanded James.

'Relent the Alpha position, give control of your pack over to me—'

'You're crazy if you think I'm going to give up on my pack. I'm going to protect them!'

The Alpha pressed harder with his revolver on James's throat, it was starting to hurt more than he could tolerate – even with his instincts healing him, the constant pressure was discomforting at best, painful at worst.

'And the other thing you're going to do,' the other continued as though he'd never been interrupted, 'is renege on the vampire-werewolf alliance.' James snorted. 'Do all that, and you'll survive, your pack will be safe in my hands, and you can run off with your merry band of vampires never to be seen again.' He paused. 'Do we have a deal?'

'No!' growled James.

With a roar, he kicked backwards as hard as he could just as the gun went off – the bullet nicked his chin just barely. James groaned at the initial pain, but his body healed almost instantly.

The Alpha grabbed James by the hair and slammed his forehead into the wall so hard, dots speckled James's vision. The revolver came to press against his cheek.

'Big mistake, James Sharpe,' his adversary seethed.

James felt himself pushed up against the wall again before someone pulled the Alpha off him and slammed him onto the floor. James spun around.

Victoria had the werewolf's arms bent backwards as she pinned him to his stomach, her skirt riding up just enough to allow her to straddle his ass and squeeze her knees against his ribs.

James lunged for his gun as the vampire expertly twisted the mystery Alpha's gunhand and divested him of his revolver. James pointed his pistol at the rival Alpha, holding it in one hand, and pulled back the safety.

His drumming heart louder in his head than the club music, James took a beat to exhale in relief. He wiped the side of his mouth with his free hand as he watched Victoria overpower the enemy werewolf – surprise and her lithe vampiric movements had worked in her favour. She was at once formidable as she was sexy.

'Get off me, bitch!'

'I don't know who the hell you are,' Victoria cooed, 'but I want you and your goons out of my club. And if you come back, there'll be hell to pay.'

The werewolf struggled but finally managed to shove Victoria off him. Victoria stood, wiping a bead of sweat off her forehead.

The Alpha bounced up and glared at her. He raised his hand to strike her and she caught his arm, stopping it firmly. The rival werewolf's eyes widened in surprise as he paused long enough for James to catch a better glimpse of the tattoos on his hands – a sun cross with an incongruent lozenge in the centre that made it look like a spearhead.

Victoria's eyes flared and she hissed at the man, canines and all. 'I suggest you take your friends and leave . . . now! I trust you can carry them out yourself.'

The Alpha sneered at her before bending and slapping the faces of his comrades. They woke with a start and stood, following their Alpha to the door as he snapped his fingers at them. It was much like the other day, snapping silent orders.

'Remember what I said, Sharpe.' The rival werewolf turned his head to look back at James. 'Best do what I told you – before you live to regret it.' He snarled. 'I'm the Alpha who's going to take you down.' He spat on the floor. 'You're a disgrace, you and your entire pack. Marrying a vampire.' He spat again before leaving.

James seethed, balling his hands into fists – his hand was wrapped so tightly around the pistol, it trembled. 'Asinine! Completely and utterly asinine!' James wiped his forehead with his quivering gun hand.

Victoria looked past James, 'Seriously?' James followed her gaze to the hole in the wall. She sighed, her eyes returning to his face. 'You okay?'

'Yeah. Thanks for the assist.' James felt a little rattled and embarrassed that he'd needed help.

'You would have done the same for me.' Victoria's voice was soft and comforting.

'How d'you know I was in trouble?' asked James.

'I heard a roar that sounded distressed.'

James nodded and holstered his gun. He sighed, steadying himself but feeling too rattled still. 'That Alpha is strong . . . and dangerous. I underestimated him. He had so many with him last time he jumped me, I thought I could take him on my own.'

'He did kind of isolate you,' Victoria pointed out.

'Yeah.'

The patter of feet alerted James to two approaching figures. Liam and Julian appeared at the door.

'We heard a gunshot,' panted Liam. 'We came as soon as we could.'

'It's all under control,' Victoria grinned, exiting the room.

'James?' asked Julian.

'It was him again,' breathed James.

'What? For real?' shouted Liam. He glanced behind, looking ready to go after him.

'He's gone now.' James waved a dismissive hand. 'Forget about it.'

'You look rough,' noted Julian.

'Yeah, well, I *feel* rough!' James snapped, talking quickly. 'I keep getting attacked by an unknown Alpha who's making asinine demands, and on top of all that, I've learnt that my husband's been sneaking out of the house in the middle of the night and keeping it a secret from me. So yeah, I look and feel rough.'

Without wanting to talk more about it, James exited the V.I.P. lounge and returned to busying himself with what needed to be done in the club.

* * *

James waited until the following night to confront Chad. He got ready for bed at his usual time, slipped out of his clothes, wearing nothing but his boxers, and then waited until he heard Chad step out into the hall.

James swung the bedroom door open and bolted down the stairs to the entrance where Chad already had his hand on the doorknob.

'Where are you going?' he demanded.

Chad froze and bowed his head, keeping his hand on the handle.

'You've been going out at night after I've gone to bed, haven't you?'

Chad slowly turned to face him. 'I've been going to think.'

'Going to think?' James leaned forward. 'Where?'

'By the river,' replied Chad. His face seemed tormented, like he was hiding something from James.

A rock formed in the pit of James's stomach – he had hoped it was simply that Chad had omitted to tell him, but from the look on Chad's face, he knew there was more to it, that it was more grave, and that Chad was deliberately keeping this hidden from him.

'Why?'

'I have regrets,' Chad said carefully.

A pang of dread clenched James's heart. 'Regrets?!' he asked shakily.

Chad spoke quickly. 'It's nothing to do with you, James – this has nothing to do with us.'

'Then what the fuck *is* it about?!'

Chad merely stared back at him.

'Chad, I'm your husband, why the hell would you hide something from me? Why would you . . . lie to me.'

'I'm not lying, I swear, James . . . I just have not told you.'

James growled, his voice low, 'Not lying, my ass.'

James glowered at Chad, his jaw tight, feeling his body tremble. He was more afraid than he was angry right now, and by the change in his husband's expression, James knew Chad recognised the anguish he'd caused him.

James crossed his arms and, his voice low, trying to keep it from shaking, asked carefully, 'Why are you sneaking out and why have you never told me that you go off . . . to think?'

'It's . . . I . . . was not ready to confront . . . I didn't want, but . . . now . . . I regret not having looked her in the eyes to ask her why.'

James realised who Chad was talking about. 'Mandy,' he breathed. He creased his brows into a scowl. He retorted, 'Why are you even giving her a second's thought?'

'Because I loved her like a sister!' shouted Chad.

Chad and James gaped at each other as Chad's eyes flared with anger. James took a step back, realising how strongly Chad felt.

'Why can't you talk to me, then?' demanded James, dismay tugging at his heart. 'Never have you once mentioned her since last year. How could I know? Why do you feel the need to keep this from me?' Fear gripped James like the twist of a knife. 'Am I that inadequate as a husband?'

'This isn't about you, James!' cried Chad. 'Just . . . let me deal with this my way, okay!'

Chad stormed out into the night and in a flash of vampiric speed, was out of sight. James cursed under his breath – he wanted to punch the wall. He rubbed a hand down his face before trudging to the living room and slumping down on the sofa, wanting only for Chad to return so they could talk.

* * *

Feeling agitated, Chad dashed with vampiric speed. He stopped to catch his breath near the corner shop where the young woman who reminded him of Mandy worked. He hesitated before going in, his hand on the handle. He had to ask himself if he was trying to replace Mandy.

'So what if I am?' he growled to himself. He pulled the door open and walked in.

'Hey again!' he was greeted by her friendly voice.

'Hey again,' he repeated.

'Neat contacts. Where'd you get them?'

'Excuse me?'

'Your eyes – glowy almost white. Really cool effect.'

'Shit,' Chad hissed under his breath.

Turning his head to the side, Chad cursed himself for not paying enough attention to ensure his nerves had calmed. He had failed to subdue his instincts. He sighed. Well, there was nothing for it – he'd let her think he was wearing contact lenses.

'Is it safe for you to work here this late?' he blurted, changing the subject.

'Okay, boomer. I can defend myself, you know. I do the half-night shift and I've always been fine. Plus, the security button is here in case of an emergency.'

'Sorry, call me old fashioned but—'

'You're old fashioned.'

'It's just . . . It's dangerous out there,' Chad pointed a thumb towards the exit. 'There are people attacking people out there.'

'Unless your name is Sharpe or you've got beef with a Sharpe, there's no problem.' She put a hand on her hip. God, did she remind Chad of Mandy sometimes.

'And if I told you my husband was James Sharpe?'

Her eyes widened, and then she grimaced. 'I think I inadvertently threw you under the bus.' Chad scowled in confusion. The girl winced in sympathy. 'I'm so sorry.' She hesitated.

'Don't leave me in suspense.'

'I was at a party at Nightly Glow, right? And a guy I was flirting with who turned me down,' she bumbled nervously, 'well, I talked about you because all the guys at the bar were hot and married to each other, and this one guy, well, he had the same ring as you and I realised after, he must be your husband, and I mentioned you going to the river and he kind of looked upset.'

She drew in a deep breath. Chad merely stared at her, mouth agape.

She shrugged, hands out. 'I guess that guy was James Sharpe?'

'It's fine. We, uh . . . It's difficult to talk about some things and we're still getting used to being newlyweds.'

'I am so sorry!' Her brows were so drawn together in a pleading apology, it tugged at Chad's heart.

Chad smiled tenderly. 'Don't worry about it. We're cool.'

Her face lit up. 'Okay, then. Also, to answer your question about your husband – I'd say, way to go, hot stuff. I mean, his muscles are on fleek!' Chad chuckled. 'Also, I just want to apologise for thinking you were a creep last time. I didn't realise you were gay. That was . . . inappropriate of me to assume—'

'It's fine. I'm pan, actually, or . . . well . . . I've been with all kinds of people. I'm sorry if I gave off the wrong signals with my word choice last time, when you thought I was flirting. I . . . tend to compliment people I find attractive.' Chad grimaced sheepishly. 'I do tend to flirt, or sound flirtatious even when I'm not flirting.' He chuckled self-consciously.

The woman gave him a friendly smirk and walked from behind the counter to face him. She held her hand out. 'I'm Paige.'

'I'm Chad.' They shook hands.

Chad felt himself relax but was careful to maintain his paled eyes for the benefit of the ruse. He grabbed a chocolate bar.

'Same as last time, I see.' Then, after he paid for it. 'Enjoy your walk by the river, assuming that's where you're headed.'

'It is. Thanks.' Chad gave her a wave.

'And again, I'm sorry if I caused any weirdness between you and your husband.'

Chad stopped in front of the door and turned his head to look at her. He opened his mouth to speak but instead, merely smiled at her and waved before exiting the shop.

Chapter Four

Dawn was already underway and James was growing more worried by the minute – he didn't want Chad to weaken from the sun, he was scared for him. James heard the front door open and he stood from his seat. Chad walked in and glanced at James.

'Chad,' James said softly.

The vampire's eyes trailed the length of James's body and probably noted his lack of clothing. 'Were you waiting for me all night?'

James merely looked at him earnestly. 'I'm sorry.'

Chad's eyes widened. 'What are *you* apologising for?'

'I didn't realise that you were going through something and I couldn't be there for you the way you needed me to be.'

Chad shook his head, taking a few steps towards James. 'James, baby, *I* should be the one to apologise, not you. I've been carrying this grief with me and I kept it from you. I'm sorry. I'm just not ready to talk about it.'

'Baby,' James closed the distance between them and passed the backs of his fingers over Chad's face, leaning his forehead against his. 'It's fine if you can't talk about it yet. But don't sneak off and hide that from me. I understand you want to deal with this your way, just don't hide it, that's all I ask. Tell me when you need your space, tell me when you feel these things. You don't have to tell me *why* you feel them, but I'm your husband, I want to be there for you, I want to know when you're hurting.'

James continued to caress Chad's face.

'James.' Chad tilted his head up and placed a gentle kiss on James's lips. 'I can do that – not hide these things from you. It's just . . . I feel guilty and . . .' He looked away, pained.

'It's okay, baby, you don't have to talk about it. Just let me comfort you when you need me to, okay?'

They wrapped their arms around each other, relishing the tender moment, but before long, Rachel and Keisuke were starting their day and the sun was rising high.

Before the two husbands could retreat to their bedroom, the doorbell rang.

'Can someone get that?' Rachel called out.

Chad dashed upstairs and tossed James his pants – James quickly half-dressed as he hurried to the door. Chad returned fully dressed, withdrawing further into the hall to keep away from the sun.

James opened the door to find a familiar man just a bit his junior leaning against the wall, his lean muscles flexing as he crossed his arms.

Clad in a sleeveless tight shirt and jacket, the man sported an undercut braided topknot of long dirty blond hair with messy braids, and he had just enough of a pinch to make his alabaster face look longer. His fingers were adorned with a few rings James knew were more dangerous than decorative. An elaborate Viking-style tattoo of Fenrir was inked on his entire upper arm – in his case, probably symbolising freedom and chaos more than strength and fearlessness – and while he was lean, he had a very strong and sexy build.

He tilted his head towards James, grinning and arching his brows above his light amber eyes. 'What's up, tough stuff?'

James smiled widely. 'What's up, lean stuff?'

The two men took a step towards each other and clasped hands before embracing, clapping each other on the back.

'Damn, Ian. It's been a while,' said James.

'I've been travelling. You know how it is, you say you'll visit so many places in under a month, next thing you know, it's been over a year.'

Ian let himself into the house as Liam and Julian emerged from their room and came down the stairs. Ian looked at each of them. He jerked his head towards the vampires. 'Which one of them's the husband?' His wink told James he was teasing – James had sent him photos of the wedding.

'That would be me,' said Chad, leaning forward and extending his hand.

Ian clasped his hand. 'Well done, Chad. Didn't think James would ever settle down.' He winked at him.

James motioned Ian to the others. 'I want you to meet Ian.'

'Nice to meet you,' they expressed.

Ian nodded to each of them as he shook their hands in turn. He pointed a thumb towards James. 'I'm his best friend.'

'Says the man who had to send me a *video* of his best man speech because he couldn't make it to my wedding.'

'I'm sorry, ok?' Ian sighed defensively, raising his hands in surrender. 'We all make mistakes'

'Uh-huh?' Amused, James widened his smile. 'And what is the name of this mistake?'

The look on Ian's face said it all. 'Eugénie . . . and her husband, François.'

'Look at you, scoring a married couple,' teased James.

'I'm curious to know what happened,' admitted Liam.

'There we were, enjoying a clandestine affair, Eugénie and I, and then one day – literally in the middle of the day – François walked in on us . . . joined us, and then he became clingy.'

'Well that sounds like trouble,' Chad teased with a chuckle.

James couldn't help but laugh. Ian had that mild nasal quality to his voice that James found so endearing, amplified when Ian was complaining. It had always made James regard Ian as a younger brother he wanted to protect, even if Ian had many a time posed as his bodyguard.

'I escaped from France to Italy,' Ian added quickly. He turned back to James. 'My mother called me in a frenzy, because *your* mother called *her* in a frenzy, begging me to return to the continent.'

'*That's* why my mother said she was sending me a package,' James realised, 'said it was worthy of the Alpha.'

Ian grinned. 'Your mom said I'm worthy of the Alpha.' He bit his lower lip before sticking his tongue out as his grin widened.

'Shut up!' James snapped playfully.

'What? I can't help it,' Ian shrugged. 'Your mom's a total milf. So's your aunt, mind you, but she's also scary in a sexy way.'

'Hence why Adrienne was the Alpha for so long,' James reminded him.

'So you're . . . ?' began Liam.

'A werewolf, yes. And a member of the Sharpe pack, though I'm not a Sharpe, not remotely related, though that's . . . kind of obvious.' He grinned at James who just kept smiling, feeling heartened. 'I'm told you need a bodyguard. So that's why I'm here.'

'My bodyguard?' James looked down at his large exposed muscles, and then at Ian's leaner muscles – they had always teased each other about their contrasting builds.

'Hey, it's no time to make jokes about that, your life's on the line, you're in danger. I'm here to protect you.' Ian pouted teasingly, 'I've been your bodyguard before, let me be it again.' He opened up his sleeveless jacket, now back to his usual enthusiastic self. 'I've got knives, darts, guns, my nunchucks. I'm good with stealth. *And* I've got exceptional speed, speed that rivals the fastest of vampires. No offence, vamps, I hear you're good, but no one's as good as me.'

'Pfft, d'you hear that?' chuckled Julian, glancing at Liam and Chad. 'He's a bit full of himself, isn't he?'

'I hear you got jumped a couple of times now by some Alpha-Alpha. Hence my return from the Mediterranean. And it's lucky you know me, it is . . . *molto bene.*' He exaggerated the Italian.

'So you've come *from* Italy, then?' inquired James.

'*Roma!*' answered Ian. Chad said something to him in Italian. 'Come again?'

'That's what I thought,' Chad chuckled.

Rachel and Keisuke came into the hall. Dressed in a professional-looking skirt, Rachel was a bundle of nerves, giving Keisuke instruction after instruction. 'Diapers are in the top drawer.'

'Yes, I know,' Keisuke reassured. He was casually dressed, yet he somehow seemed to look prim and proper. His hair fell neatly by his shoulders today.

'It's Rachel's first day at work after her maternity leave,' Liam explained to Ian, 'and Keisuke's first day of paternity leave.'

'They married a few months after Liam and Julian did, and Rachel gave birth last fall,' explained James.

Rachel turned to Ian. 'I heard the word "bodyguard." You going to be staying here, then?'

'Can he?' asked James.

'Yes. I'll add you to the roster.' She smiled at Ian.

'Ooh, roster. Sweet.' Ian rubbed his hands together. 'Roster for what?'

Everyone stifled laughs as Rachel answered, 'Poopy duty.'

Ian crinkled his nose. 'Wonderful,' he muttered, a hint of sarcasm in his tone.

Rachel hurried to the door; Keisuke trailed behind her holding the baby. She kissed Hikaru's head before Keisuke passed him to Liam.

Holding one of her hands close to his heart, Keisuke cupped Rachel's cheek. 'Rachel.' He brought both his hands to her face, holding her gently. He kissed her long and tenderly, though it looked very steamy – from this angle James saw their tongues.

Keisuke pulled away slowly. 'I love you,' he whispered.

'I love you.' Rachel blushed and lowered her voice, though they all heard her very clearly. 'But you can't kiss me like that in front of my brother, Kei.'

'Oh, but you can kiss her like that in front of the others so they can still ogle at you both,' Liam piped up.

'I certainly like the view of both of them,' Ian said under his breath, grinning and crossing his arms.

'Not another one,' sighed Rachel. 'Okay, bye. Behave.' She pointed at Ian. 'Follow the house rules, they're on the fridge.'

'Have a nice day!' Liam called out. Rachel waved again and hurried out the door.

Keisuke sighed loudly, smiling wistfully. Then he took the baby back from Liam and turned to Ian. 'I'm

Keisuke, Rachel's husband. It's nice to formally meet you.'

'Likewise.' Ian looked from Keisuke to the vampires, and then back at James. 'So, like, is one of the house rules to be married or something?' joked Ian. 'And . . . rules on the fridge?' There was a hint of surprise in his voice.

James beckoned for him to follow and they all entered the kitchen.

'We all put effort into contributing to rules we'd all agree upon,' explained James, pointing towards a nice piece of stationery that was stuck to the fridge with magnets. 'I suggest you pay close attention to applying number five.'

'Wait, what?' Ian took the paper from the fridge and read the rules over in his head. 'No slovenliness! Only cleanliness!' He exclaimed. Hikaru seemed amused and bumbled happily in Keisuke's arms, pointing at Ian. 'What *is* this?'

James laughed and Hikaru laughed some more.

'The baby likes you, Ian,' smiled Keisuke. He looked down at his son. 'Don't you, Hikaru?' His tone was always so formal, but it had a playful air to it now. 'Smile for daddy . . .' Keisuke dipped Hikaru playfully and the baby shouted excitedly.

'Hey, if I'm going to be staying here,' began Ian, 'can I have a say in these rules too?'

James only laughed even harder. 'We're equal shareholders of this mortgage. Actually,' James grinned, 'seeing as I'm a Sharpe by name, I put the downpayment. If you want a say in the house rules . . .' James beckoned with his hand. Then, closing it up as though demanding payment, 'Pay up.'

'You've gotta be kidding me!' complained Ian. 'You own a million-dollar house!'

'The perks of having a Sharpe as a roommate,' said Keisuke, flashing Ian a smile – Hikaru mumbled inaudibly in his arms. 'And to having a vampire brother-in-law, I suppose.' He placed his finger on one of the numbers on the list. 'Memorise this list, learn the ropes, because my wife is going to ensure you know it by heart. Now follow me, I'll show you where we keep the diapers.'

'For real?' Ian gaped after Keisuke who didn't wait for a response but simply walked over to Hikaru's room.

'Should've stayed in Italy,' James muttered, chiding playfully. Ian flipped him the bird before following Keisuke into the baby's room.

* * *

In the end, James, Chad, and Keisuke spent much of the morning and part of the afternoon showing Ian around the house and putting him up to speed with everything that had been going on. Later, Keisuke stepped out to make Ian a copy of the keys while Chad pre-pared them some lunch.

Now, finally, James and Chad retreated upstairs for some much-needed sleep.

They sat in bed – the sun behind the thick drapes indicated it was late afternoon, the time on James's watch confirmed it. James let himself fall back onto the pillow. 'Oh, I am beat!'

Chad chuckled and lay down beside James, taking his hand in his. 'Ian is a handful, isn't he?'

James laughed. 'Yeah, he's so rambunctious. Oh, but I love him to bits.'

'He's your childhood best friend.'

'Yes.' James chuckled. 'He has a lot of energy.'

'Keisuke was acting like he was taking care of *two* children back there,' remarked Chad.

'That human's awesome. He's a good father.' James stifled a yawn. 'Wow, I feel like I could sleep through the whole night till morning.'

'Same here.'

'I didn't sleep a wink last night,' said James.

Chad turned his head to him and tightened his grip on his hand. 'I'm sorry I caused you so much distress, James. I promise to be a better husband to you.'

'Chad, baby,' James turned onto his side, his voice like the tender caress he wanted to convey, 'you don't need to be a better husband, you're already the best husband I could have hoped to have. We're both learning to be the best husbands we can be for each other. We'll make mistakes, but we do our best – that's all I ask.'

Chad smiled wanly. 'James, I promise to uphold my oath to the pack. I will live up to it and be the best Partner-Alpha they could expect me to be, so I can be as worthy as you of the honour.'

James's heart tugged sweetly. He cupped Chad's face, one hand trailing the side of his arm. 'See, this is why I love you so much, Chad. This, you wanting to be worthy of the pack . . . It means so much just to have you as my lover, let alone my husband. You accept me, all of me.'

James briefly thought back to his exes, and to some of the assumptions he'd made due to past relationships, and then how wrong he was proven when Chad joined him during Feral Night.

'It's one thing for a human to accept who I am, but a *vampire!?* And you love me. *I have your love.* Every day I'm amazed by it, by just how much you love me and by how much I love you.'

Chad's eyes furrowed tenderly – James could get lost staring into those dark eyes of his.

'What an unlikely pair we are,' James expressed. 'And every day, I am so thankful that you fell as much in love with me as I did with you, even if you said you needed things to be casual at first. I was so scared when you said that because I had already fallen for you. I fell in love so fast, Chad.'

Chad blinked and his eyes sparkled with tears, and it only made it harder for James to keep his in.

'And then, when I promised you I'd do everything for us to be together, even if that meant leaving my pack, you got down on one knee and asked me to marry you.'

'You were willing to abandon your dream for me. I needed you to know I was willing to be part of that dream for you.'

James and Chad both let out tearful laughs. 'The love I feel for you, I feel it so deeply. It drives me crazy sometimes,' admitted James.

'I feel the exact same way, James.' Chad's voice was gentle and comforting. Chad smiled wistfully. 'I had already fallen for you too, James. My fear of losing you . . .' Chad shook his head. 'But I was already a lost cause, mad for the werewolf who drove me insane with sensations words can't describe.'

James's heart swelled. 'Thank you,' he whispered.

'What for?' asked Chad.

'For existing,' replied James. Chad drew in a quick breath. 'For being in my life. For loving me. For . . . everything.'

'Thank you, then, for your devotion to me, for your caring.' Chad kissed James tenderly. He kept his lips close as he continued. 'Having your love, having this – what we have together – it makes the millennia of . . . it makes me becoming a vampire worth it. It makes my then new forced existence worth it. It . . . it makes it *all* worth it.'

The two kissed again, pressing their lips together and breathing tearfully, but merely keeping the kiss at that.

James chuckled. 'Look at us, middle-aged sappy men, on the verge of falling asleep, making declarations of love to each other all over again. If I weren't so tired, I'd *show* you those declarations.'

'You say middle-aged as though it applies to us,' Chad chided teasingly. 'I'm as ancient as they come, the millennia keep stacking up! And you're probably double the age you look, what with your lifespan. Middle-aged men, my ass.'

'You mean to say you don't intend to live another three thousand years?'

'I mean that I'm so young, middle-aged can only apply after ten thousand years.' Chad let out a laugh.

James chewed his lip. 'You didn't respond to my declaration of wishing I had the energy to make love to you.'

'I'm beyond tired.' Chad's voice was nonchalant, though his smile was playful. 'I'll react when I can respond in kind and show you how a husband fucks his husband good.'

'Hmmm,' James sighed, his voice throaty, 'that's more like it.'

James wrapped his arms around Chad and closed his eyes as the two fell right to sleep.

CHAPTER FIVE

The lavish grand halls of the vampire manor towered above Chad as he strode through them.

'Chad!' the familiar voice called behind him. He turned to find Mandy jogging towards him. She wrapped her arms around him in a tight bear hug.

'Oof!' Chad chuckled. 'What's brought this on?'

'Do I need a reason to hug you?'

Chad smiled, feeling warmth in his heart. 'No, I suppose you don't.' Smiling, he reciprocated the gesture, holding Mandy close to him.

* * *

Chad awoke abruptly, his muscles jerking and heart beating at a hundred miles per hour. James beside him stirred. With the hand that was on Chad's chest, James caressed him gently. Chad took a few deep breaths. Outside, it was dark – Chad could only assume it was the middle of the night.

'Baby?' James murmured groggily, still half-asleep. He lifted his head as his eyes focused on Chad. 'What's wrong, baby?'

Chad heaved a sigh. 'It was just a dream.'

'Hey,' James cupped Chad's face, the gesture reassuring, 'I'm not going to let that Alpha and his goons get the better of me. I promise.'

'I know. I'm not worried about that. I . . . dreamt of . . . her.' Chad met James's eyes. 'I don't understand. She was being affectionate with me. It was . . . a memory. But she . . .' Chad stopped himself from saying the rest.

James nodded his understanding. 'She was being a hypocrite.'

'Part of me wants to believe she cared about me, even if she wanted to exterminate us all,' sighed Chad.

'If she did care about you – and *genuinely* cared – would it make her betrayal hurt any less?'

'No,' Chad declared dryly, his voice grave. He stared up at the ceiling, feeling his heart beat in anger.

'Baby, it's okay. I'm here.' James hesitated. 'Do you want to talk about it, in fuller—'

'No.' Chad turned and leaned his forehead on James's, the ache in his heart squeezing. Chad's voice trembled. 'I just want you to hold me, James.'

James wrapped his strong arms around Chad and pulled him closer. Chad nestled into James's embrace, breathing in his scent and closing his eyes, wanting only to feel content.

* * *

'So what's on the agenda?' Ian asked as he got into the passenger seat next to James.

James sighed internally – he hated leaving Chad at home knowing he was feeling down after that dream, but James had Alpha duties he had to stop delaying. It was best he get an early start to the day.

'Go talk to some important members of the pack, see some important allies, that sort of thing,' he told Ian. 'I've got to speak with everyone now that I'm the Alpha, get an idea of where everyone's at.'

'Yeah, but weren't you already doing that?'

'Yes, so this is no different, except more official since it's the first time I'm doing the rounds *as Alpha.*' James powered on the car and pulled out of the driveway. 'I've also got to stop by the club for some paperwork, but that can wait till later.'

'Bo-ring.' Ian sing-songed. 'But okay . . . You're the boss.'

James and Ian visited many pack members, old friends and Sharpe allies – not just werewolves, humans too – all who knew James was now Alpha. Most of it was formal small talk, while others invited them in for a bite to eat or for some tea or coffee. Some of the guys from the pack were glad to see Ian again and alluded to wanting him to join their poker nights, just like before his trip. It amused James.

Many visits and several hours later, James and Ian were well-fed by the time they arrived at the club. These so-to-speak meetings had taken the better part of the day.

Now James sat pensively at the manager's desk in Nightly Glow's office, poring over the books and the roster – both the physical papers and the spreadsheets on the computer – reorganising a few things to ensure all was in order. Victoria took care of a lot of it too; however, since last year – since her turning – she could no longer come in during the day like she used to.

Reopening Nightly Glow had been one of the best decisions James had pushed for after the whole debacle, but it had meant more responsibilities at certain times of the year – for the quarterly reports, to be precise, and James hated leaving it to the last minute.

Dressed in his usual denim, this time with a long-sleeved jacket, Ian sat across from him on the other side of the desk, quietly fidgeting and looking around the office, hands on the armrests. James could tell he was bored.

He looked up from his papers. 'Thanks by the way, for coming to help. I know it cut your trip short.'

Ian waved a dismissive hand. 'I can always go back and visit the countries I missed later. You're in danger now. Your life's more important than a tour around Europe.'

James felt heartened. 'That means a lot.'

'I'm your childhood best friend, you think I wouldn't drop everything and get my ass here when it mattered most? What kind of friend would I be, James!'

James nodded, smiling his appreciation, then shook his head, rubbing his forehead. 'That Alpha, man, I don't even know his name.'

'Yeah, well, the next time he dares show his face, I'll be there and ready to take him on,' declared Ian.

'He's strong – stronger than me,' James cautioned. 'I might have large muscles, but he's got hyperstrength.'

'Yeah, but I'm agile.' Ian smirked with pride. James knew he was in good hands.

James studied his friend carefully. 'It means a lot to me that you're okay with the alliance with the vamps, you know. It . . . would have been awkward otherwise.'

'Duah.' Ian grinned. 'Adrienne personally called every single pack member to ensure we were okay with it before proceeding to make it official. She told me what happened – in *her* words. I didn't just hear it from you when you called to tell me you were engaged to a vampire and how that happened.' Ian leaned forward on his chair. 'You know what I said to her?' James cocked a brow. 'Well it's about damn time.'

James laughed. 'It's true, you were that pup in the pack who wanted to be friends with all the beings of the Underworld and didn't understand why we were carrying old grievances that happened before we were even born.'

Ian nodded. 'From what I hear, anyone who had reservations got to personally speak with Keisuke.' His eyes widened. 'He's gooood. He even got me to enjoy playing with the baby.'

James chuckled. 'Hikaru's a little bundle of joy, isn't he?'

'How does she do it – Rachel, I mean – living with only men?'

'You read our house rules, did you not?' reminded James.

'No slovenliness, only cleanliness,' Ian muttered, disgruntled. James burst out laughing. Ian sobered. 'You really love him, don't you – Chad, I mean?'

James put his pen down. 'I love him more than I've ever loved anyone in my life. He's everything to me and I'd do anything for him.'

Ian's smile was warm. 'I'm glad to hear it. Perhaps someday I'll find someone who makes me feel that way too.'

James grinned, wanting to poke fun at his friend. 'You'd have to start by being a bit more disciplined.'

'Hey,' Ian scowled, 'I can be disciplined!'

'Says the man who's earned himself a reputation for being the pack's rebel werewolf,' James retorted boyishly.

'Yeah, and who do you think taught me that? Mister I'm-Marrying-A-Vampire, even if they're a werewolf's sworn enemy.'

'All right, all right, you got me there.' James laughed and returned to the papers. Then, he proceeded to enter the data into the computer. It was part old-school filing and part modern tech filing, and that's how the Sharpes did it to ensure there were no errors – or when they needed to hide anything. They were, after all, a mafia, not just the leading family of a leading werewolf pack.

Ian fidgeted again, tapping his fingers on the armrests and bouncing his leg up and down annoyingly fast.

James sighed. 'You started smoking again, haven't you?'

Ian opened his mouth to speak, then grimaced. 'I may have picked up some bad habits while touring Europe.'

'Why didn't you say so!?'

'You're the one who helped me quit the first time, practically barricading me! I thought maybe I could go without again, once the plane touched down on the continent, but . . . I guess I'm having a harder time of it than I thought I would.'

'It happens.'

James continued his work in silence for several minutes.

Ian piped up again. 'Hey, by the way, congrats on getting Chad to commit to you! I hear he wasn't much of a long-term commitment type nor the monogamous type.'

James felt his cheeks become warm. 'So that's what you and Keisuke were talking about while Chad and I slept.'

'Among other things.'

James paused what he was doing, seeing Chad's face in his mind's eye, missing him and wishing Chad could be here with him now. He always missed him the moment they were no longer in each other's presence, and he knew Chad felt the same.

'I think his love for me did that for us,' James answered Ian. 'We would have made it work – I would have been willing to consider it for him – but once all needs and emotions were expressed, Chad only had eyes for me. He's the one who proposed too. I feel so lucky.'

'He's the lucky one, James. You're a heartthrob. *And* the Alpha. And now a vampire's our pack's Partner-Alpha? Wow! Times really have changed – *you've* changed – and it's all been for the better.'

James merely smiled, heartened that his best friend felt this way – it meant so much to him. He did his best to refocus on the task at hand while he completed entering the numbers. When he was done, he pushed his chair back, glancing down at his watch.

'Right, okay,' Ian said before James could announce their next destination. 'We need to stop by somewhere I can get something to smoke.'

'That's fine.'

James closed up behind him and the two werewolves stopped by a corner shop near the club so Ian could get what he needed.

They stepped out of the shop and Ian flicked his lighter open with a clink and lit up the cigarette dangling from his mouth. He took in a deep drag.

'Oh, sweetness!' he said, exhaling the smoke, and immediately his fidgeting stopped.

James chuckled, taking his phone. 'Hey baby,' he said as soon as he heard Chad's voice. 'We're still on the other side of town and I don't know when I'm going to be done my rounds.'

'Text me your location at sundown and I'll join you,' Chad immediately replied.

'I'd like that. All right, let's do that. I love you, baby.'

'I love you.'

Biting his lip, James hung up and put his phone back in his pocket.

'Oohhhh, you're so in love,' Ian teased him. James's face felt hot. 'Bet you he makes you howl and growl and roar into the night.'

James playfully shoved Ian as the two continued towards the car.

* * *

Chad dashed with vampiric speed to the park where James told him to meet him. He saw James and Ian on a park bench. James was leaning forward and had his arms resting on his knees. Ian had his elbows draped over the back of the bench and was looking up at the sky, exhaling a lazy cloud of smoke.

Chad arrived in a flash before them and Ian's eyes widened.

'Whoa!' he coughed, choking on his smoke. 'A little warning next time.'

'Sorry. I was eager,' admitted Chad. James stood and pulled Chad to him, holding him tightly.

'I'll give you two some privacy.' Ian stood and retreated. Chad could no longer see him, but the smoke from his cigarette drifted towards them with the wind and he could smell him close by.

'I missed you today,' said James.

'Yeah?' Chad smiled. Every time they expressed such emotions, his stomach whooped.

'It was a long day and I just wanted you by my side.' James had a twinkle in his eyes. 'And I wasn't the only one. Many of the pack members said that next time I do my rounds, I should come at night so that you can accompany me.'

'Really?' Chad looked down, uncertain of the emotion he felt, but he knew it was a good one.

James placed his fingers beneath Chad's chin and tilted his face up to meet his gaze. 'Yes, really. The pack loves you, Chad. Just not as much as I love you, of course.' They both chuckled. 'There are still a few people left to visit. I'd like you to accompany me.'

'I'd like that,' replied Chad. He felt butterflies in his stomach. 'Oh, wow,' he breathed. 'I feel just as nervous as when I met your parents.'

James beamed at him, taking his hands in his. 'It's going to be fine. They'll be so happy to have their Alpha's husband visit them.'

'It would be an honour to accompany you.' Chad let out a one-breathed nervous laugh. 'James, baby, this is amazing, the things you make me feel all the time.'

Feeling giddy, Chad leaned forward and kissed James tenderly.

'Then perhaps later we can get to what we were talking about doing yesterday,' whispered James, his voice husky.

It was true, James's early dart had not allowed for them to indulge in their passion, not to mention Chad had been feeling out of sorts after that dream. But the reminder of his husband's desire ignited something within him and Chad felt like his entire body was on fire.

'Then let's get those visits done so we can get on with it,' Chad urged, admiring his husband's face with the lust he felt for him. James chuckled.

'James?' a female voice called out from nearby.

Chad and James stepped apart to turn to the voice's owner.

A beautiful woman in her thirties approached them, beaming in astonishment. Her long curly hair was flawless and she looked like the type who took great care of her appearance. 'James Sharpe?'

'Olivia?' James exclaimed, wide-eyed. Chad could only observe the interaction, feeling awkward as he sensed history between them.

'Oh my god, James, it's so good to see you.'

'Is it?' James asked, looking sheepish.

Olivia sobered. 'Yeah, actually, it is.' She looked at Chad and with her eyes prompted James for an introduction.

'Oh, uh, Chad, this is Olivia – we dated several years back.' Chad nodded his understanding. 'Olivia, I'd like you to meet my husband, Chad.'

'Husband, eh! Settling down now, are we?' Smiling, Olivia extended her hand to Chad.

'It's nice to meet you, Olivia,' said Chad, shaking her hand.

'Well, I'm engaged,' said Olivia, showing a lavishly ornate ring with a large diamond at the top. 'We're in town, visiting my folks for the week. I'm on my way to meet my sisters at a bar. He's – Benton, my fiancé – entertaining my father with a cigar and some brandy.' She let out a small laugh.

'You're happy?' asked James.

'Yeah, I am.' Her smile radiated. 'He's a top dog, that one.'

'When you say "top dog . . ."' began James.

'He's a football quarterback,' replied Olivia. She took out her phone and showed them a picture of her with a muscular man, arms around each other, standing before a lavish house. 'That's me and Benton.'

'Is that your house behind you?' inquired Chad.

'Yeah.' Olivia put her phone away again.

A silence fell. Olivia and James looked awkwardly at each other. Olivia pressed her lips together nervously.

'Listen, I'm glad you found someone to share . . . you know . . .' Olivia said. 'Look, things might have ended in heartache for both of us but I still care about you, and I'm happy to see you happy, James.'

'Same here.'

Olivia looked from Chad to James. 'I know I chose not to be part of your world with you, but I hope you're keeping safe. Is, uh, is he part of that world too?' Chad was unsure what she was implying – for all he knew, she might have been referring to the mob life.

'Yeah, he is,' replied James.

'Then everything worked out for the better,' declared Olivia.

'Actually, he's,' James laughed nervously, 'he's a vamp.' So Olivia knew about the beings of the Underworld, then, Chad concluded.

Olivia's mouth dropped in shock, but behind it, she wore a smile. 'I thought you wanted to kill all vampires!'

'Yeah, I thought that too . . .' James beamed at Chad, clearly unable to suppress his grin, '. . . before I fell in love with one of them.'

Olivia smiled again. 'Listen,' she pulled out a piece of paper and wrote on it. 'I know things sometimes get dicey in your line of work. If ever you need a safe place to lie low, this is where I am now.' She handed James the paper. 'I know it's a few hours out but . . . you know.'

'Olivia, I can't ask you to risk yourself like that. This . . . was the reason you said you couldn't stay with me. There are . . . dangers – I've got a rival.'

'No one will know, except the two of you. And, well, it's not like I'm getting involved in all the dangers. Besides, I got my permit to own a gun now and I keep the silver close by. Honestly, if you're ever stuck, as a last resort, no one would expect it, so it would be safe . . . for all of us.' She glanced at Chad. 'I can only imagine the shit the two of you might fall into just from your union.'

James passed a hand through his hair. 'You have no idea, Olivia.'

Olivia reached for James's face before catching herself. 'I mean it, I still care about you. If you're ever stuck . . .' She smiled in empathy. 'And I'll hide the silverware.'

James chuckled. 'Thanks.'

'I should, uh, get going,' said Olivia, her smile warm. 'It was nice seeing you, James. And it was lovely to meet you, Chad.' She gave them a small wave and walked away.

James heaved a sigh.

'So she knows,' noted Chad.

'Yeah, she knows what I am.' James met Chad's eyes. 'Sorry I never told you about her. I was pretty broken up about it at first, but . . . she didn't want to be part of this life, the dangers of the Underworld. When we broke up, we still loved each other.'

'Does part of you still love her?' asked Chad. James eyed him carefully. 'I ask only because I know how I still feel about all my past loves, even if that love changed and I no longer am *in love* with them – well some of them at least, the ones I still love are dead.'

James worked his jaw nervously. 'I'm not going to lie to you, Chad, I still care about her. That's why we should throw this out.' He said, waving the piece of paper with Olivia's address on it. 'She should stay out of this life. She chose not to be a part of it. My duty as an Alpha of the alliance is to protect her.' He looked down at the paper. 'I won't force it on her. I care too much about her for that.' James met Chad's gaze anew. 'But I am no longer in love with her. The only one I truly love is you, Chad.'

Chad smiled, reassured. 'I know.' Though it helped to hear confirmation from James. He took James's hand in his, starting to walk with him. 'And . . . thank you for being honest with me.'

James smiled back, looking awkward still, but Chad trusted him and understood how he felt. Together they walked to the car where Ian joined them, literally stepping out of the shadows. Chad had momentarily forgotten the other werewolf was shadowing them. And then they proceeded to complete James's rounds with some friendly visits to pack members who were thrilled to officially and personally meet Chad.

Many weeks passed, and spring blossomed into summer. Several negotiations had taken place between vampires and werewolves who had travelled from afar to speak with James and Chad – Keisuke had assisted the pair.

Many packs and covens had travelled to also meet the 'fabled' *Sui Generis Lamia,* as many had dubbed him. Chad teased Liam that he was a *fabled* being now. It amused him.

Stella, Wilbur, and Richard always conducted themselves in exemplary fashion in the face of arguing vampires and werewolves, and James and Chad showed a united front, their union either said to be inspiring or appalling.

Despite some negotiations ending with either side needing more time to think – thus breaking Keisuke's perfect streak – many more were signing the agreement for the alliance and were willing to take the necessary next steps.

Chad remained impressed with how much help Keisuke was in their talks, how diplomatic he always was. Chad had been training him as well, in some combat arts – those Chad had learnt many centuries prior during the time he had lived in Japan. Now the human walked around with a *wakizashi* strapped to his back, the one given to him on his wedding night the previous September, the one that had belonged to his ancestor.

'Oof, things got a bit dicey back there,' remarked James, turning around to walk backwards as the group of friends strolled out into the street after another meeting.

'That's why you have me,' boasted Keisuke.

'No kidding,' said Liam. 'It's a good thing. Those vampires from up north were amenable to the idea, but the werewolf pack . . . eesh. They kept turning down all their offers.'

'Oh, but they had Cuban cigars,' sighed Ian. 'Gosh, they smelled so good. It took all my self-control not to ask them to give me one.'

James chuckled.

'But those vamps were kind – they even brought cookies,' laughed Chad. The pastries they'd brought were undeniably delicious, *and* homemade – those were always the best.

'They were patient,' noted Julian. '*I* would have lost my cool way sooner.'

'Did you see how Wilbur stared down that pack's Alpha like a champ?!' exclaimed Chad with a chuckle.

'Did you see how Adrienne whooshed her hair in his face like she was the Alpha-Alpha?' said James. 'I'm telling you, my aunt sometimes scares even me. But I'm glad she assisted in this one. Her relationship with that pack goes a long way and it meant a lot that she was there as a show of respect, even if she's no longer the Sharpe Pack Alpha.'

'And when that other Alpha said, "Your Alpha married a vamp!"' began Ian.

James imitated Adrienne. '"That vamp is more of an Alpha than you'll ever be and has earned his place in my pack."'

They all laughed.

'It *was* impressive,' admitted Keisuke. 'Though it did make things a bit tense for a bit.'

'We got there in the end, didn't we?' Julian reminded him, spreading his arms out in a half-shrug.

'*I* got us there in the end,' Keisuke specified, 'thank you very much.'

'Oh-ho, don't let it get to your head!' Liam teased, nudging his brother-in-law with his elbow.

'Too late for that, I think,' muttered Chad.

He and Keisuke exchanged a laugh.

'Something sounds amusing,' a deep and menacing voice proclaimed. A large group of men approached them from all sides. 'Care to clue us in?'

James stopped and spun around, his shoulders tense, and he immediately adopted a defensive stance. That's when Chad realised who this man walking towards them was. His heart palpitated in sudden fear and anger. He took a steadying breath, ready to defend his husband from the werewolf Alpha threatening him.

'You!' James glared at the newcomer, backing away.

Ian stepped up beside James, ready to pounce. Julian and Liam stood close together, and Chad found himself standing back to back with Keisuke as James squared off with the other Alpha.

They were surrounded and outnumbered.

Chad had to wonder if this werewolf was the leader of his faction or if . . . *she* still existed and was its leader.

'It's been a while,' stated the Alpha, cracking his knuckles. 'Thought it was time I paid you a visit, check in on how much of our deal you're upholding.'

'I made no deal with you,' growled James. 'I told you, I won't abide by your asinine demands. You can shove them up your ass.'

The Alpha chuckled mirthlessly. 'I don't think you're in any position to argue against me.'

His werewolves – all men – looked ready to pounce or had their hands on their weapons. Right now, stalling them for answers seemed a viable option, and if Chad knew his husband's mind well, he knew that was what James was going to try to go for.

Chad glanced at the Alpha's hands and his heart dropped to his stomach. It was the symbol of the *Argenteae Hastae*, the *Silver Spears*, led by the woman who had once seduced and abused Chad.

Chad looked up and noticed more beings approaching slowly, joining the werewolves surrounding them – vampires. Chad was puzzled, but his thoughts did not linger on why or how vampires and werewolves were working together in opposition to a vampire-werewolf alliance.

Behind him, Keisuke was trembling, his breathing and heart rate were erratic.

Turning his head to the side to glance at his friend, Chad asked in Japanese, keeping his voice low, '*Do you remember what we practised?*'

'*Do* you *remember what we practised?*' Keisuke replied in kind.

'*I* am *the one who trained with Samurai,*' Chad reminded him, keeping his tone conversational.

'*I am the one who's Japanese by blood.*'

Chad and Keisuke chuckled. Good – Keisuke's breathing was one of a focused warrior now and he no longer trembled.

'Thank you,' Keisuke whispered.

'I'm not stepping down as Alpha,' James declared. 'Nor am I giving up on the alliance. And I am *not*—' he took a menacing step forward, 'leaving my husband.'

That drew Chad's attention back to the Alphas.

'Last time I thought you might agree to run off into the sunset with your vamp-tramp of a husband—'

'Don't you *dare* insult him like that,' seethed James. Chad clenched his hands into fists but said nothing.

'But seeing as you're being difficult,' the other Alpha continued, 'perhaps it's best you two went your separate ways. Better for my objectives, anyway.'

'*Argenteae Hastae!*' Chad declared, turning to face the man, who narrowed his eyes at Chad. 'That is the symbol you wear on your hands. The Silver Spears.

You are a pack Alpha but you are not the leader of the Silver Spears.'

'And how would you know that, vamp?' retorted the werewolf.

'Constantia,' breathed Chad. 'She lives, doesn't she? And she leads you, doesn't she?'

Something in the man's expression told Chad he was correct. But then his eyes flared and Chad was alerted to the subtle movement of attacking werewolves.

As one, the small group of vampires and Sharpes moved defensively against the werewolves who lunged at them. Keisuke crouched low, hand on his short sword, and pulled it from its sheath on his back. He slashed at a werewolf's legs as Chad kicked another away.

They had to fight strategically. If they killed any who were of the opposing kind – a vampire killing a werewolf or vice versa – it would undo all the progress they had been working towards. Nor could they kill one of their own kind unprovoked, especially not when the situation was so delicate. Doing so would make them outcasts. If they did not draw the necessary lines in the face of violent opposition, then who would?

Hence, Liam, Chad, and Julian contended with fighting the vampires of the group, while Ian and James fought the werewolves, and Keisuke simply fought to remain unharmed, whoever attacked him, but Chad remained close by him – this was, after all, the human's first fight of this nature.

James roared and Ian sent a dart at a werewolf. The two Alpha's locked arms, shoving against each other, teeth bared.

'You know how this is going to end, James Sharpe,' proclaimed the Alpha.

'With my gun against your throat!'

'With *mine* against yours!'

A werewolf tried to bite Ian's arm off and he stabbed him with a small knife. The werewolf whimpered, staggering away. Chad surmised, by how the man was wincing, that Ian had used a poisoned knife, one that would make healing difficult, if not temporarily subdue the ability altogether.

Ian pulled out a *nunchaku* and pulled the two sticks apart, revealing a metal chain. He hopped onto the Alpha's back, hooking his arms over the man's shoulders and bringing the chain above his neck to choke him. The rival Alpha bent forward with such force, Ian was propelled off him and landed on his back, skidding on the pavement.

'Shit,' Ian cursed.

Ian rolled over in time as another werewolf plunged towards him, claws ready to tear him apart. Ian retracted his nunchucks before producing another knife. He flicked it at the werewolf who caught it in the neck. The werewolf gurgled, but merely plucked the knife out, the lesion healing almost instantly, even as blood spilled from his neck.

Ian cursed again.

Julian jumped up and dashed a vampire who came at his neck, teeth ready to bite him. He shoved him off, but the enemy vampire pounced at him again, hissing, and nearly getting him this time. Julian fought him off non-lethally as long as he could, but his opponent was relentless and dove in for the kill. Just in time to save his own life, Julian punched through him, sending his guts spraying onto the pavement.

Keisuke sliced diagonally at a vampire coming at him as Liam pulled the attacker away and up against the side of a parked car. Liam drew his dagger and placed its point nearly touching the pinned vampire's throat. The vampire yelped and raised his hands in surrender.

'You see what this is?' demanded Liam. 'Do you *all* see?'

Vampires and werewolves turned to look, distracted by the silver dagger.

Ian and Julian took advantage to grab hold of the mystery Alpha. James pinned him to the ground onto his stomach, digging his knee into his spine. He unholstered his pistol and pressed it against his enemy's head. Keisuke brought his *wakizashi* to rest against the Alpha's throat.

Immediately the werewolves took defensive stances but stopped all fighting or attempt to fight. It was as James had described to Chad, they stopped when their Alpha was in danger but remained alert to defend him.

Weapons were trained on James, Ian, Julian, and Keisuke, but the werewolves knew, like James had said they had during that first attack, if they attacked, their Alpha would be killed. Thus, none made the next move.

Chad merely remained where he stood, defensively near Liam as backup.

'You know what this is,' Liam sneered in a conclusive tone, bringing the attention of all back to him. 'Answer my questions and I'll let you live.'

'You'd kill a fellow vampire?'

They had already killed some of their attackers, it was too late to regret any action that might impede on the progress of the alliance and the amends either kind had been making. That being the case, Chad knew, if they could prove this was an enemy faction, they'd be justified and in the clear, and their duty would then become to protect the alliance and its members from this enemy at all costs.

'Fellow implies you're on my side, not trying to kill me – so yes, I'd kill another vampire.' Liam's eyes flared. 'I am, after all, the one who killed She-Who-Betrayed-Us. You remember Mandy? Who tried to get mere mortals to kill vampires and werewolves alike?'

'They should've killed you all off, your coven *and* the Sharpes,' the vampire sneered.

'Don't say anything that'll give us away,' the Alpha warned.

'I observe vampires and werewolves working together,' James disdained, his gun pressing even harder against the other Alpha's temple, 'and yet you told me you were against the alliance.'

'Hypocritical, if you ask me,' remarked Chad, letting his anger seep into his voice. He remained alert in case anyone attacked again, but for now, the fighting had paused. The attention of all was on Liam's silver dagger and on the pinned Alpha.

'Why are vampires and werewolves who oppose the alliance working together?' demanded Liam. When no answer came, he brought the tip of the dagger closer to the vampire's throat.

'We're temporarily united for a great cause,' the vampire yelled. 'We're purists.' He pointed towards James and Chad. 'Your pack and coven are tainting vampires and werewolves. You will only spread your taint worldwide.'

'Is that what you think?' demanded Liam. 'That we're going to make it all worse? How is peace worse than war?!'

'Don't answer that!' the Alpha commanded, struggling beneath James. 'Or I'll let him kill you if you do. You're expendable, vampire.'

Liam let go of the vampire and took a step back. 'Fine. Don't tell me. But we'll learn the truth soon enough.'

The vampire lunged at Liam, and in the momentary surprise, ripped the dagger from Liam's grasp. Liam cried out as the vampire slashed his entire side, from shoulder down to his stomach.

Liam's eyes flashed angrily, his face contorted in pain, and he rammed the vampire against the car so hard that it dented. The knife fell free of the vampire's grasp. Liam lunged for it, spun around 360 degrees, and stabbed it down into the vampire's gut.

Inky tendrils snaked around the vampire's stomach. He began to gasp and spasm as the infection spread. Liam twisted the knife, his face reflecting his rage.

'Answer me and I will make this quick and painless.'

'Shut it!' the Alpha bellowed in command.

The wound on Liam's side had drenched his clothes in blood, but Chad knew it had already healed itself by now.

Liam again twisted the dagger and again and the vampire grunted in pain before his body went limp. Liam pulled the dagger out, letting the dead vampire crumple to the asphalt, and spun towards the werewolf Alpha, pointing the blood-soaked dagger in his direction as blood dripped from its tip.

'We heard the rumours, but I did not believe them to be true,' the Alpha muttered. 'A *Sui Generis Lamia* stands before me, and you're on *their* side?' He raised his voice. 'You're with those who would mix blood and allow impurity to trickle down the generations?' He screamed at Liam. 'You should be with us! Fighting for the purity of what you are, of what you represent!'

Liam took a menacing step towards the Alpha, his expression growing cold, the dripping dagger still levelled.

'Tch, you would kill a werewolf? Do that and you reignite our war. So come on, kill me, then.'

James, Ian and Julian continued to hold the other Alpha, while his pack members and vamps began to take steps back.

'Run away, then, you cowards,' the Alpha growled.

'No, you stay!' commanded Liam. 'And watch.'

'Liam?' Chad warned, reaching for his arm to stop him. Liam flared his bright green eyes, widening them momentarily, and Chad let go of Liam, understanding his intent.

Liam crouched and took the Alpha by the wrist, turning his palm upward. He placed the flat side of the dagger on his wrist. The werewolf screamed as his skin began to turn black beneath it.

'Tell me your name,' demanded Liam.

Chad shifted uneasily, but he nodded to James. He trusted Liam knew what he was doing.

Liam pressed the dagger harder. The Alpha grunted and his face twisted in agony.

'It's Troy,' he panted. 'I am the Alpha of my pack and the contender to lead the werewolf division of the Silver Spears – a faction of werewolves, vampires, and fae, ready to fight to keep our people separate and pure.'

'Contender,' James pressed.

'Another leads it, but if he is eliminated or disgraced, I rise up to take his place. Something I hope will happen without me needing to lift a finger.'

Chad took a step towards him. 'And Constantia?'

'Yes, she lives and leads us,' replied Troy, with growing effort. His entire hand was beginning to turn jet black now.

'The Silver Spears, a name meant to represent the very things that kill creatures and beings of the Underworld,' said Chad, staring down at Liam's dagger, the very dagger that had killed Mandy. 'It all began with a group of vampires who believed they would destroy the impure, would act as the silver poison to those poisoning the purity of their kind mixing with werewolves and fae.'

'You know your history, *Chad Sharpe*,' Troy growled, wincing. The way he'd spat Chad's name . . . the ancient vampire was uncertain whether Troy was insulting his marriage to James or insinuating he knew of Chad's history with Constantia . . . or both.

'And if you've spent any time in Constantia's presence, then you know that she knows me, that I was there during that time.'

Chad was urged by a desire to know more, but if Liam didn't do anything about Troy soon, the poison would spread and kill him.

As if James knew too, he gave Liam a warning. 'A *werewolf* should finish him off, not a vampire. He's *mine* to kill.'

Troy glared at Liam. 'Now you've gone and done it. Word will spread that you've killed a werewolf Alpha, here in the territory where there is peace between werewolves and vampires.'

'Who said anything about me killing you?' Liam rebuked.

Liam removed the dagger from the palm of Troy's hand and spat on Troy's wrist. Immediately the Alpha's skin began to turn pink again and the relief was apparent on his face.

Liam backed away from him. 'Tell your *Argenteae Hastae* that the *Sui Generis Lamia* healed you of a silver wound. I never intended to kill you, Troy, only to learn your purpose.' He thrust his head forward in contempt. 'Now go. We won't be so merciful next time you decide to attack us.'

James nodded to the others. Keisuke took a step back, sweeping his short sword away. Julian and Ian let go of Troy, and James got off him, keeping his gun levelled just in case.

Troy stood on unsteady legs before backing away. He laughed sinisterly. 'Should've killed me when you had the chance.' His eyes landed on James. 'You're going to live to regret it, James Sharpe.'

And then he was gone, bounding away, and so were the werewolves and vampires who followed him.

All present exchanged glances with one another. 'Everyone okay?' asked James.

Julian walked to Liam, bringing a hand to the gash. 'I'm fine,' Liam assured. 'It hurts like a bitch every time, but I'm okay.'

Keisuke let out a long breath and sheathed his *wakizashi*. 'Let's go home.'

CHAPTER SEVEN

Still reeling from the encounter and by what it had revealed, the group of men made their way back to the mansion. Chad found his mind drifting to his past with Constantia.

James was still reeling from his fight with Troy, and Keisuke was far too calm for someone who'd just been in his first life-threatening altercation. Ian kept literally hissing, and complaining that he should have been better at defending James – James repeatedly told him he had not failed as his bodyguard. Julian and Liam walked side by side, whispering to each other, grim expressions on their faces.

They had staked the dead vampires and let their ashes drift in the breeze – they did not want any bodies to be found. Ian had scoured the place for any hidden security cameras – thankfully, he found none. The rain that had slowly begun would wash away the blood. Thus, the only evidence that remained of the struggle was the dented car – whoever owned it would be severely disappointed. Nevertheless, Ian had lock-picked the car with expert ease, and James left a stack of cash on the passenger seat, having stated, 'That should cover the cost of repairs.'

Chad brought his attention back to his friends as they walked up the path to the door.

'Well, if rumour wasn't spreading fast that a *Sui Generis Lamia* lives around here, now it will,' Chad voiced. 'And they'll know that you possess a silver dagger.'

Liam unlocked the door and they all filed into the house, leaving their shoes by the door. They proceeded to grumble about the events as they settled back in.

'I just can't believe the hypocrisy of it all,' exclaimed Julian. Chad was with him on that front.

'Hypocrisy of what?' asked Rachel as they entered the kitchen.

She sat with a woman whose back was facing the group, but Chad observed she wore a brown leather jacket and flexible tight black denim pants. Her black hair, primarily straight with intermittent waves, cascaded just below her shoulders on either side of her face. Delicate hands of an olive complexion were wrapped around her teacup, as she and Rachel sat sipping tea. She did not turn to face the group. A baby monitor sat next to Rachel's cup on the table.

'Who's this?' Liam asked with suspicion.

'Made myself a new friend,' replied Rachel, giving the woman a knowing look.

'Oh, a mother from the breastfeeding group?' asked Julian, taking a few more steps into the room.

'No, this one knocked on the door a little over an hour ago,' replied Rachel.

'You let a stranger into the house!' hissed Liam. The others gathered around, taking protective stances.

The woman stood but kept her back to them. 'I must apologise for the intrusion.' Chad recognised her accent as Argentinian.

Rachel's eyes landed on her husband, and her face fell. 'Keisuke! There's *blood* on your *wakizashi.*'

Keisuke shifted uneasily. 'That Alpha attacked us.'

'What?!? And you're only sharing that with me now?' Rachel stood and hurried to Keisuke's side, fussing over him.

'I'm fine,' Keisuke reassured.

'This is why I have come,' their guest declared. The woman turned to face them for the first time since their arrival. Even with her face devoid of make-up, she radiated beauty, with naturally lush pink lips and dark eyebrows just the right thickness to make her hazel eyes stand out.

'Wow,' whispered Ian.

Chad took a step towards the woman, recognising her allure right away. 'You are fae.'

'That is correct.' The woman tucked her hair behind her ears, revealing pointed ears. She gave them a formal smile and nodded. She looked to be the equivalent of someone in her late twenties if Chad had to guess – fae matured differently, seeing as they were millennial beings. Chad reckoned this fae was close to five hundred years of age.

'Whoa, okay.' Liam relaxed somewhat.

'You may call me Rayan.' Her eyes surveyed the vampires and werewolves before her. 'There is growing dissent among certain vampires, werewolves, and fae; the ancient faction of the purists is revived.'

'Ancient faction,' repeated Liam. 'You mean the Silver Spears?'

'Sí. That is correct,' replied Rayan.

'The only other time beings of the Underworld banded together was to ensure the purity of each,' said Chad, repeating what he had once shared with the others. 'It ended in bloodshed for all, including the fae people who retaliated against us before the truth was known. Fae were banished into their realm and disallowed to roam the realm of the mortal-living for centuries.'

Rayan nodded 'The Silver Spears wish to destroy whatever progress you have made in reconciling werewolves with vampires. We fae wish to see peace finally come to the world and all its realms between all our peoples. That and . . .' Her mouth rose to a side smile. 'I wished to meet the *Sui Generis Lamia* in person.'

'You're shimmering,' observed Liam.

While Chad had recognised her essence, he had no doubt that Liam could detect more about the fae.

Rayan's smile widened. 'You see my three forms, yes?'

'I see this form, but it's shimmering.'

'Ah, so not quite like fae perceive each other, then,' noted Rayan. 'We see the embodied form but always perceive all our forms through the lens of our magic.' She grinned. 'We fae embody two tangible forms, and one luminescent form. While outside the Fae Realm we cannot fully embody our true fae form, we all possess the ability to switch at will between our female and male forms.'

Rayan fluctuated momentarily and now before them stood a man in his late twenties, his long hair giving him quite the allure. His thick eyebrows on a now more forward façade seemed to make his gaze more intense. Faint hints of stubble speckled his face on his square jaw and around sultry lips. A fae's forms always mirrored each other like twins might.

The fae grinned, taking a step towards Liam and cocking his head to the side.

'Yes, you like this form, don't you?'

'Uh,' Liam hesitated.

'I see a few of you prefer this form.' Rayan's amused grin was enticing.

Julian stepped between Liam and Rayan. 'I prefer the form that doesn't come on to my husband.'

Chad snorted in his throat. He leaned forward and whispered in an obvious manner. 'He's the jealous type.'

'Ah, noted.' Rayan took a step back, showing under-standing. *Mis disculpas,*' he added, though a playful smile tugged at the corners of his mouth.

'I must admit, I like both forms very much,' Ian expressed.

Chad chuckled. 'I must agree that both forms present their unique qualities.'

James playfully slapped Chad's arm with the back of his hand. 'And I'm still not agreeing to sharing you with anyone.'

'Not suggesting that, just paying a compliment.' Chad said, raising his hands in defence.

Rayan chuckled. 'I was not expecting to be this amused by you. If it's easier for you, how is this?' Rayan coruscated back to female form with a shimmer and smiled at the group. 'You'll soon discover that my qualities include lithe flexibility in this form and vigour in the other. I have unique skills and have received rigorous training,' explained Rayan.

'Of course, this is mostly aesthetic,' the preternatural being added, a coy smirk playing on the side of her lips. 'Though we do enjoy the pleasures that come from all our forms.' Rayan chuckled. 'I could show you my true fae form but you wouldn't be able to perceive me, not here anyway.'

'I've been to the Fae Realm,' Chad commented, 'and there I could perceive fae in their true forms. It is as you describe, beyond anything words can convey or anything our non-fae minds can comprehend.'

Rayan's eyes darted to Ian, who seemed to suddenly remember to swallow his saliva, slurping it in loudly. 'So do we refer to you as . . .' Ian trailed off – the intensity of Rayan's gaze was enough to render anyone speechless.

The fae smiled slyly. 'You may refer to me as she when in this form, he in the other. It is as we fae refer to each other as well when presenting tangibly.'

'And when you're in your true fae form?' inquired Ian, inclining his head to the side.

Rayan grinned widely, locking eyes with Ian and coming to stand nose-to-nose with him. 'When I am in my true fae form, then you may call yourself fortunate to have had the privilege to marvel upon the magnificence of my true form.'

Ian exhaled, passing a hand through his messy braids. The energy between them was palpable.

Everyone else took a beat to take in what their new preternatural friend was sharing about the fae and their realm.

'Okay, so you want to help us?' James asked cautiously, bringing the conversation back to the issue at hand.

'That is correct,' asserted Rayan, turning to the Alpha. 'Many of my people want peace between the three peoples, unlike the purists. I am here because we wish to join your alliance, so that fae can help you as we once did.'

'I have a concern,' voiced Julian. 'Is it safe here now after . . .' He pointed a thumb behind them.

'Troy, the Alpha attacking me,' said James, 'tonight wasn't the first time nor will it be the last that he ambushes me, and he had vampires with him this time.'

'Oh my god,' whispered Rachel, bringing a hand to her mouth.

'We fended them off,' Keisuke said in a reassuring tone that sounded a bit strained, 'but I'd be lying if I said I didn't fear for my life in that moment. I want to stay alive and I want to stay human.'

'Understandably,' Rayan nodded, compassion in her eyes.

'We also learnt that their true leader is the very same vampire who led them centuries ago,' said Chad.

'I have learnt of Constantia,' nodded Rayan. 'Then she still lives.'

'It appears so,' replied Chad, dismayed.

'So back to my question,' Julian interjected, 'after all that back there, and you being here now, is the house safe?'

'I have already used my magic on this home – at Rachel's behest.' Rayan and Rachel exchanged a meaningful look. 'She allowed me to cast a protection around it. You are safe on the terrain of this house. It exists as any fae home does now, protected and hidden from those who would seek to harm it or anyone within it. Your enemies cannot approach this residence uninvited without hitting a magical barrier that will be more painful to run into than you.'

'Thank you,' sighed Liam. 'We appreciate that.'

The legends were partly true about supernatural beings and entering homes unless invited. Any home protected by magic repelled enemy beings unless they were explicitly invited into that home. Supernatural friends and allies could at any time enter, with or without such protections. That the mansion was now thus shielded was reassuring, to say the least.

'When Rayan first arrived, she introduced herself to me and explained her purpose for being here,' said Rachel. 'I don't know if it was her magic that did it, but I just knew I could trust her.'

'It is her magic,' Chad confirmed. 'While some fae are good at concealing their magical energy, most permeate their intentions. Many can only be perceived thus by other supernatural beings. Rayan's essence is strong, I have no doubt you felt it.'

'All right,' said Liam, 'so the house is safe, my sister and nephew are safe, we're all protected here, but . . .' Everyone knew the question on his lips.

'That still doesn't help us deal with Troy,' growled James. 'You heard him back there – we should have killed him when we had the chance. But that's not how honourable werewolves do things.'

'We wanted answers and we got answers,' Ian pointed out. 'Hopefully, now that I know his tactics firsthand, I can better protect you next time he decides to make an appearance.'

Chad raked a hand through his hair, concern tugging at his chest. 'I can't help but wonder if Constantia is trying to hurt me for what I did to her.' He looked at James. 'What better way to hurt me than to eliminate the man I love.' He blinked back tears, stung by the betrayal *he* lived all over again. 'I know what betrayal feels like. I know, even if she knew I might not truly join her, what she must have felt when I chose my coven over her.'

'But Troy has his own agenda,' James reminded him. 'He wants me to *give* my pack to him, and for me to rescind my induction to Alpha. He may be aligned with Constantia to hinder the alliance and the peace we're brokering between vampires and werewolves, but he has his own designs, his own goals, and he wants to be the dominant Alpha in the new world they are creating.'

'It's as though he hopes that werewolves will come out on top when it's all over,' Ian surmised, playing with his pinch.

'I can bet my bottom dollar that their new plans don't involve letting humans live in peace,' seethed Keisuke.

'So what are we going to do about it?' asked Liam. 'We're not going to stop negotiations. And if there's anything I can do as the *Sui Generis Lamia,* I'm open to it.'

'Right now, you may lie low and proceed as usual,' Rayan advised. 'I will return to my realm and report to the Fae High Council. I will be back. I want to show you all that the fae people can be trusted and that we want to be part of this alliance.' She locked eyes with Keisuke. 'You can prepare the paperwork and I will sign with your pen and embed it with my magic. Please, include me in your alliance as the first fae to sign with you.'

'I will prepare the necessary materials for your next visit,' confirmed Keisuke.

'Thank you. I appreciate you putting your trust in me thus. I promise to honour that trust and to uphold my part of our new alliance.' Rayan smiled, eyes roaming each of them before stepping back.

'I'll show you out,' said Rachel.

'*Gracias*, Rachel. You are very kind.'

James sighed. 'What a night.'

* * *

James sat on the edge of the bed, removing his socks as he undid his belt. He sighed – he couldn't stop sighing. The adrenaline had left his body, leaving him feeling unnerved, and nothing their new ally had said had given him any reassurance. They were no closer to dealing with their immediate danger.

'You're worried,' Chad observed, removing his pants.

James tried to smile. 'Everywhere we go, everyone around me . . . Keisuke could have gotten hurt real bad back there.'

'He knows how to defend himself,' noted Chad. 'Plus, we've been showing him and Rachel how to fight off vampires and werewolves more effectively.' Chad smiled in sympathy. 'He held his own in that fight.'

'Maybe, but he shouldn't have been in that position to begin with.'

Chad walked over to James, unbuttoning his shirt and exposing his sleek chest. He was in nothing but that open shirt and his boxers. It was almost enough to make James forget every-thing else.

'Besides,' Chad continued, 'the house is protected with fae magic now.'

James passed a hand through his hair. 'I suppose.'

He looked up at the face of the man he loved – the man he had married – the vampire's beautiful curly hair falling on either side of his ears as he peered down at James. Letting himself succumb to his primal urges, James set everything else aside in his mind.

James grabbed Chad's ass and reached his mouth up to nibble on his pecs, letting out a guttural growl. Chad moaned and grabbed onto James's shoulders, pulling on his tight top to remove it. Letting go of Chad,

James crossed his arms and lifted his short-sleeved shirt over his head to toss it aside before going back for more nibbles.

'Oh, James, baby,' Chad sighed loudly, as James's teeth grazed his stomach.

James slid his hand under Chad's boxers, pulling them down and his mouth engulfed his erect cock. It pleased James to see that his outburst of desire had turned his husband on this instantly.

'Fuck, James!'

Chad rocked gently back and forth as he stood before James who sucked gently at first. James looked up as he plunged his man's length deeper into his throat, his stomach flipping elatedly – it turned him on so much to pleasure his husband. Chad tilted his head back, biting his lower lip to suppress a shout. A moan still escaped his lips, which only made the arousal in James's groin harden.

James reached into his pants and pulled out his own erect length, stroking himself as he continued to devour his husband. The heat rose in his body tenfold as the touch of his big hand quenched part of his need.

Chad's eyes darkened before they flared and his canines extended. He licked his thumb and his hand found James's, taking over the stroking. He rubbed his wet thumb over James's plump shaft and James groaned onto Chad's cock.

James pulled back, looking into Chad's eyes. 'I want your ass to ride me.'

He kissed the tip of Chad's shaft as his hands glided along the vampire's pecs and down his abdomen. Then he turned him around.

'Fuck me, then.' Chad's husky whisper made James's cock pulse a few times.

James had to control himself before he could insert himself, else he might come right away – just teasing Chad's opening was enough to make James experience a pre-orgasm orgasm.

James kissed his man's sleek and hairless ass, nibbling as he stroked Chad's cock. He loved the hairless behind, but loved the unshaven look on Chad – he so loved a man with pubes – and tonight he was relishing it all.

James pushed gently so Chad would lean forward just enough so James's tongue could reach his anus and lick his entrance, making it nice and wet for him. James spat into Chad's ass, his tongue dancing along hungrily. He knew the natural roughness of his werewolf tongue would drive Chad up the wall – sometimes it did so literally

'Oh my god, James, baby, just fuck me already,' moaned Chad. James chuckled – Chad's most sensitive spot and his favourite position was James inside his ass.

James pulled away. 'Yeah, you ready to ride me, baby?'

'I'm so ready to fucking ride you, baby. You ready to fuck this vampire of yours?'

In response, James pulled Chad into a sitting position on top of him and his large erection slid right into him, slowly and smoothly.

'Fuck,' Chad and James both breathed together.

James growled in his throat, burying his face in Chad's shirt to stifle the sound. Chad began to bounce up and down.

'Ride me, baby, fucking ride me,' James commanded.

Chad bounced as James stroked him, he could feel both their cocks stiffen.

'Oh my god, your ass feels so good, baby,' whispered James. 'It's so fucking tight.'

'You think it's tight now?' taunted Chad. He pushed further and James fell back onto the bed, his feet still touching the floor, and Chad's rectum closed tighter around his dick.

A shout escaped James before he could stop it, and the room spun around him as he felt his face hotter than a fire launcher. He rose to bury his face in Chad's neck, pumping his husband. James stifled a scream as he came inside Chad.

This sent Chad over the edge, as the vampire gave a soft shout and spurted up all the way over his shoulder and onto James's face.

Wanting to give Chad a proper finish, James lifted Chad's ass and pulled out in one swift motion. He bounced onto his knees as Chad fell back onto the mattress. James hovered over Chad, his face upside down to his.

He kissed his mouth from this position, enveloping his lips with greed and need, before licking whatever semen had sprayed already, all the way down to his pelvis, and then engulfed him into his mouth anew.

'Fuck!' Chad cried, as James sucked him hard. He knew Chad wasn't done, and he sent his cock as deep as it would go, fighting the gag reflex as he sucked even harder.

James's mouth was quickly filled with the warm salty taste of Chad's fluid as the vampire dug his nails into James's back, jerking his legs and moaning before a final elated sigh escaped him.

James pulled him out, licking him clean and swallowing whatever remained to swallow. He kissed him again before repositioning himself to kiss him upright.

Chad wrapped his arms around James, moaning into his mouth, but even now as James kissed him and relished the tender moment after having made love to him, his worries flooded his mind once more and a pang jolted his heart.

There would always be those opposed to an alliance and truce between vampires and werewolves, and because James was an Alpha, that rode more dangerously and heavily on his future and that of those around him. Because of that, Chad would never be safe, their lives would always be strife with danger. And the thought that Chad's life could be in danger because of him, hurt James more than anything else ever could.

CHAPTER EIGHT

James dressed quietly as Chad slept, and kissed him on the cheek before going downstairs for some breakfast. It was already close to midday. Ian was lounging downstairs, his braids just as unruly as ever.

'Ian, get yourself ready, we have business to attend to.'

'Yes, sir!'

After a quick but hearty breakfast, the two were ready for the day. The doorbell rang and Ian went to answer it.

'Why, hello again,' he said flirtatiously.

James walked over to find Ian leaning an arm on the wall as he admired their guest. Rayan stood on the other side of the threshold, in male form, clad in simple denim pants, a white t-shirt and a thin leather jacket. Sunglasses hung at his shirt's collar and he wore a purple fedora that concealed his ears while letting his hair fall stylishly to either side of his face.

'You're back soon indeed,' Ian went on. He crossed his arms and not-too-subtly puffed out his chest. 'Eager to see me again?'

James suppressed a laugh.

'Actually, I'm here for James,' said Rayan, smirking playfully. His eyes travelled the length of Ian's physique before he sobered, turning his attention to James.

'And what can I do for you?' asked James.

'More what *I* can do for *you*,' replied Rayan. His lips curled into a prideful smirk. 'I've returned to pose as your bodyguard, James Sharpe.'

'Oh, uh,' began Ian, 'that's fine, he's already got a bodyguard.'

Rayan arched his brow, sizing Ian up and down. 'Who, you? Pfft, please.'

'Excuse me?' Ian exclaimed, looking affronted.

'In my care, you will be kept safe,' Rayan assured James. Ian's face contorted with all sorts of emotions. James could only stare at him amused.

'But *I'm* his bodyguard!'

'You obviously weren't able to protect him very well last night,' Rayan remarked. 'The *Sui Generis Lamia* had to step in.'

'To be fair,' offered James, 'we were outnumbered. That is how Troy gets the upper hand – always. And then we were able to overpower him, everyone together.'

'Well, with my protection, you won't have to worry about being outnumbered.' Rayan swished his hair back, looking very slick. 'I have fae abilities that will ensure your safety.'

'That's very kind of you,' began Ian – James detected a hint of hurt ego – 'but he doesn't need another bodyguard. It'll draw too much attention.'

'Actually, I don't mind having both of you tag along,' James interjected. Ian gawked at him. The truth was, the thought of having double the protection offered James much reassurance, especially after last night.

'But I'm your best friend!'

'Having such a title as *friend* does not necessarily give you the ability to protect him as he should be,' Rayan stated dryly.

'As he should be? What is this?' complained Ian. 'What happened to the flirty, eyelash-batting Rayan from last night?'

'I told you, I enjoy both my forms and each offers unique qualities. Today I'm posing like this.' Rayan gestured, sweeping his hand downward in a self-revealing motion.

'Well, I mean, you look good and all, but I'm the one who's James's bodyguard,' insisted Ian.

'Will you just let it go,' sighed James, exasperated. 'Have a smoke, I think you need one.'

'What I need is not to be undermined by a fae we don't even know!'

As if on cue, Keisuke arrived at the entrance foyer from down the corridor, papers in hand. 'I *thought* I heard you arrive. I'm sure my friends will feel more secure of your presence after you've signed the agreement I've printed out.' Keisuke gave Ian a pointed stare.

Ian frowned, tapping his foot on the floor, arms crossed. He pouted but said nothing as Rayan read and signed Keisuke's documents.

James glanced over at the contract and noticed the emblem on the top corner of the page. 'That a triskelion?' he asked.

'Yes,' replied Keisuke. 'Triskele, as it's sometimes referred to, symbol of trinities. I figured now that the fae are signing into the alliance, it was an appropriate symbol to incorporate, and seeing as our enemy has an emblem of their own – a heraldry, as it were – I figured why not have one of *our* own.'

'Nice.' James nodded his approval. 'Good choice.' The triple spirals of the Triskelion indeed represented their alliance. The symbol itself was Celtic in origin and represented various trinities, among other meaning.

Rayan flicked his finger over his signature. The papers glowed momentarily. 'There – imbued with magic. The deal is sealed.'

'Great,' said James. 'Now let's go. I'm sure Keisuke doesn't want us arguing here and waking Hikaru up.'

'Oh, he's playing right now,' said Keisuke. James inclined his head forward. 'Oh, right, yes, best you leave now.'

'Come now, pup,' taunted Rayan, a glint in his eyes, 'if you want to protect your *best friend*, I'm sure I could teach you how to be a *proper* bodyguard.'

Ian's mouth fell open and he dropped his hands to his sides. James suppressed a laugh as Keisuke snorted in his throat.

'You insipid fae!' exclaimed Ian.

'Me? Insipid?' laughed Rayan. 'Says the werewolf who wasted his time in Europe on meaningless affairs.'

James wondered, 'Did Rachel tell you about that?'

'We shared *much* over tea last night,' Rayan confirmed.

A sly smile crept onto Ian's face. 'If I didn't know any better, I'd say you were jealous, Rayan.'

'*No digas tonterías!* As if I'd want to get in bed with you, let alone give my heart to you.'

Ian leaned forward, grinning tauntingly. 'I'll remember that the day I seduce you.'

'Careful, pup, you've got drool on the side of your mouth.' Licking his lips seductively, Rayan reached over and wiped the side of Ian's mouth with a finger. 'Best keep your tongue in and your mouth shut.' Rayan smirked in triumph.

James and Keisuke exchanged a glance – these two were totally flirting with each other.

'Yeah, wouldn't want you to get too turned on imagining this werewolf tongue licking you.' Ian suggestively flicked his tongue in the air as though he were licking a very specific part. 'Werewolf tongues give the most pleasure.'

'Licking me is the last thing I want your tongue to do,' retorted Rayan.

'Oh? What *do* you want my tongue to do?' demanded Ian. Rayan sighed. 'Ooooh, cat got your tongue, fae?'

'Will you two give it a rest!' complained James. 'Let's get going and get shit done. And while we're at it, we can try to gather Intel on Troy and Constantia. You can flirt in the car.'

'Who's flirting?' both Rayan and Ian rebuked at the same time. They quickly turned their heads to scowl at each other.

Keisuke chuckled as he waved them off. James raised his eyebrows at his bodyguards. Something told him this was going to be a long day.

'Ian's the one who's flirting,' insisted Rayan as they all got in the car. '*Es ridículo.*'

'You're the one licking your lips and looking at me with those eyes of yours, knowing full well it's turning me on!' complained Ian.

'I'm turning you on?' inquired Rayan from the back-seat, unable to conceal the hopeful surprise in his tone and expression.

'Ahaa!' Ian shouted in triumph as James pulled out of the driveway and drove away. Ian angled himself better to face Rayan from the front passenger seat. 'You wouldn't care to know that if you weren't hoping to seduce me.'

'Oh, please, I'm just amused by how much of a pup you truly are, panting with your tongue out at me. I'm probably the first fae you've ever seen in your life.'

'So you'd rather I not be attracted to you, then? I'll just flirt with whoever I see on the street, then.' Ian lowered the window.

'Are you seriously going to cat-call someone?' James cried out. 'Seriously, Ian. Tuck it in.'

'It *is* tucked in!' Ian shot him a glare. 'Wouldn't want Rayan to lose his composure upon seeing my perfectly erect—'

'Enough!' shouted James. 'Either get a room and get it out of your systems, or shut up – both of you.' He calmed his voice. 'And Rayan, if you're planning on staying with us, you'll have to read the house rules—'

'Sí. Rachel showed them to me last night and I've memorised them.'

'All of them?' Ian gaped at Rayan. 'Already?'

'Every single one,' replied Rayan, his tone a little too emphatic to *not* be condescending.

'Figure out taking turns in the guest bedroom *now*, I don't want you arguing tonight when I'm trying to sleep.' James took a beat. 'We've got some rooms downstairs we can rearrange to be bedrooms, but it's not as lavish or bedroomy as the official bedrooms.'

That seemed to get them quieted and thinking . . . for just about thirty seconds.

As James had predicted, the two returned to insulting each other with hidden flirts as they argued over who would sleep in the official guest bedroom's bed tonight and what system to devise from here on out. James sighed, but let them get it all out of their system while they were still in the car – he expected them to behave once they stepped out.

* * *

When James came to bed, he told Chad how he only found out that Troy and his pack had been travelling throughout the territories, trying to overtake other packs, but there was little else he had learnt.

'We'll find out more in time,' replied Chad, his mind clouded by his past with Constantia from centuries ago. Chad sat on the edge of the bed beside James, but the vampire, as opposed to the werewolf, was fully clothed.

James looked him over. 'You're not coming to bed, are you?' Chad bowed his head. 'Are you going to the river to think?'

'Yes.'

Chad considered inviting James, but he wasn't entirely sure he was ready to bring him to the place he'd made his own, on those rocks on the edge of the water.

Chad offered his husband a reassuring smile. 'I promise I'll be careful and stay safe.' James nodded. Chad hesitated. 'Thank you for understanding . . .' He hesitated again, not entirely sure how to finish that.

James took Chad's hand in his. 'Just promise me to share your feelings with me when you're ready.'

Chad promised him again and reassured him tenderly, kissing him just as sweetly before he stood and left the house, leaving his husband alone in their bed.

As soon as Chad opened the door to the corner shop, he was greeted by Paige's friendly voice. 'Hey, babes.'

'Hi.' With a side smile, Chad walked straight to the counter, grabbing his usual chocolate bar and placing it on the counter.

Paige smiled at him. The more he came here on his way to the river, the more he realised how different Paige was from Mandy, even if she had some similarities, and Chad was glad of it. Somehow, chatting with her helped him deal with the grief he'd been suppressing.

Paige's face changed as a group of young men sauntered into the shop. She sighed. Chad turned to get a good look at them.

'Paige!' one of the lads called out. He had a side part cut and looked like the ringleader of his group. He leaned forward on the counter, not even heeding Chad. 'Give us some smokes.'

'You're underage, Dean,' replied Paige. 'You know I can't do that. You might've been able to slip into that club, but I'm not selling you any smokes.'

'It's just a question of a couple of months, Paige. Come on!'

'No, Dean. Besides, this gentleman was here before you. Wait your turn.' She gave him one of those bitchy smiles; Chad suppressed a laugh.

'Fine, then give us a kiss.' Dean puckered up.

'No, Dean, not interested.' Paige rolled her eyes.

'Are you seriously turning me down right now? Don't tell me you still have a crush on that nerd roommate of yours. I'm so much fitter than him.'

'Take the hint, pal,' Chad said in warning, turning to Dean. 'She said no.'

'What are you, her dad or something?'

'I'm warning you.' Chad hated guys like this kid, thinking they could walk all over whomever they chose.

'Uh, Dean?' one of the other lads muttered. 'I've seen this guy around, and you'll never guess who with.'

Dean sized Chad up and down. The kid was shorter but he had guts – Chad had to give him that. 'An old man like you doesn't scare me.'

'Forty isn't that old,' retorted Paige, 'Or . . . thirty-five?'

'Forty is accurate,' Chad replied quickly, his eyes always on Dean. He thought about his actual ancient age and what he *should* look like – when he became a vampire, he had regained a more polished allure – but it didn't matter at the moment.

'Dean, I've seen this guy with James Sharpe – you know, the mobster who took out the Cromwells in that big shootout last year?'

The mention of it jolted Chad with a pang. It always did.

Dean began backing away towards the door, still sizing Chad up and down as though he could take him on. Paige stepped out from behind the counter, hands on her hips. 'And don't come back,' she called out.

'What d'you say to me?' Dean marched back to her, getting right in her space. Paige sidestepped before he could grab her and pushed him away from her. Dean lifted his arm, ready to strike – Chad grabbed him by the wrist, stopping him before he could go any further.

'Don't even think about it, pal,' Chad seethed.

Dean's face contorted. 'Ow, you're hurting me.'

'Good. Now listen to your friend. Because I'm James Sharpe's husband.'

Dean put on a brave face, glaring at Chad, despite his predicament. 'What-evs,' complained Dean, elongating the word.

Chad gripped Dean harder, pulling him in, and lifted him by the collar. 'What did you just say?!' he raged. It took everything for him to control his primal instincts and keep his eyes and canines in check.

'Yeah, okay, fine,' a panicked Dean blurted.

Chad realised, then, that when the lad voiced the expression Mandy had so often uttered, all the rage Chad had for what she had done, he was ready to unleash it on this unmindful lad.

Chad released Dean who backed away quickly, bumping into one of his friends.

The shop door opened and in walked a man who looked to be thirty. He was dressed casually and sported a neat and thin goatee that emphasised the dimples on his umber face. His build was lean yet muscular.

As soon as he saw the lads, his face grew stern. 'Oh for the love of . . . Dean, I told you not to come back here.'

The man grabbed Dean by the collar and dragged him out of the shop, shoving him away from the door.

'Who's next?' he threatened.

Dean's lackeys hurried out of the shop.

The man looked at Paige. 'You okay?'

'Yeah, Chad here was helping me.'

The man sized Chad up. 'You a friend?' Chad confirmed. 'Thanks. I'm Kevin, the manager slash owner, and here to take over the rest of the shift.' He smiled, and Chad noted how his dimples gave him that handsome allure.

'Right on. Be right back, gentlemen.'

Paige stepped into a backroom and Chad made idle chit-chat with Kevin, who was mostly complaining about

Dean and his friends. Then Paige emerged, changed and ready to leave.

'See ya!' Paige waved at Kevin, who waved back, offering them another stunning smile.

Chad and Paige stepped out of the shop, lingering there for a moment. Chad glanced her way as she thanked him again.

'I guess old-fashioned comes in handy.' Paige pursed her lips, shimmying her shoulders with a shrug. She was adorable, and it heartened Chad to have her with him.

'Say, would you like to accompany me to the river?'

'Sure!'

They began down the sidewalk before Chad stopped. He looked down at the chocolate bar in his hand. 'I just shoplifted, so to speak.'

Paige burst out laughing, the laugh high in pitch, and she held her stomach. 'Don't worry about it. You're so funny sometimes, especially with your sophisticated accent.'

'I do not have a sophisticated accent,' argued Chad. Wilbur and Richard were the ones with the accents. 'My speech is just . . . refined.'

Paige giggled. 'Come on.' She grabbed Chad by the elbow, looping her arm through his, and the two resumed. 'So, does your husband know you've made friends with a young woman nearly half your age, or should I be worried that he'll get the wrong idea if he sees us together?'

'Why do you sound like you're hoping to run into my husband?' Chad gave her a sidelong glance.

'Because he's hot! Because you're hot too.' She let out a laugh. 'But I'm not coming on to you,' she added quickly.

'I know that. To me, you're like . . . my old friend, but different.'

'You say she betrayed you before she died. What happened, if I may ask?' Paige's eyes reflected compassion.

Chad decided to tell her a portion of the truth. 'That shootout Dean's friend mentioned? She was helping the other mob to try to take us out.'

'Ouch.'

'I trusted her.' A pang hit Chad right in the heart. 'Because of her, people I cared deeply for died.'

'I'm sorry.'

They continued in silence. When they reached the river, Chad stood on the large rocks, looking out at the horizon. He breathed in deeply, a whirlwind of emotions overwhelming him.

'Since it happened – the whole debacle – since we moved into our new home, I've been coming here, contemplating my life. Looking out at the horizon and reflecting on everything that happened recently.'

'You seem sad.'

'I am. I mean, don't get me wrong, I couldn't be happier with James or more in love with him, but . . . I think I wasn't letting myself process my feelings completely. I cared for Mandy so much. Her betrayal hurts so badly. I want to hate her, but . . .' Chad shakily exhaled his chagrin.

'At the same time you grieve her death,' concluded Paige.

Chad nodded.

'Listen, I don't know what happened at that shoot-out, and I don't know what got her killed after she betrayed you, but it's okay to feel what you feel – that maybe she deserved it, and it doesn't make you a bad person. But also to wish she was alive, and that doesn't make you a bad person either. It's okay to allow yourself to grieve her death.'

Chad reflected on Paige's words. He would flirt and diffuse any tense situation to forget his fears – he had always been like that. It was how he coped. It was his way of casting his immense grief aside. He had lost so many people dear to him because of Mandy . . . but he had also lost Mandy.

Chad closed his eyes and began to weep silently. Paige said nothing but took a few steps away and sat down on a large rock, respecting Chad's need for space.

After several moments, Chad wiped his eyes and returned his focus to Paige, who was gazing at the horizon.

'Thank you,' he said softly. Paige turned her head to him. 'For helping me come to terms with the grief I'd been bottling up all this time.'

She smiled brightly – she was the sunshine he'd needed. 'This the spot you always come to?' Chad nodded. 'Thank you for sharing it with me. Thank you for trusting me.'

Chad smiled mildly. 'We should go.'

'Aw, but the sun's gonna come up soon.'

Chad stopped himself from giving that as his reason. 'James will wonder where I've been if I'm gone too long.'

He offered his hand to Paige and helped her stand. 'And yes, I've told him about you.' He chuckled. 'He was a bit jealous at first – well, concerned – but he trusts me. I have committed to him, and I *am* committed to him.'

Chad allowed himself to regard Paige, letting his eyes roam her body before smiling. 'If I were single, I'd already have swept you off your feet. That's why I think that nerd roommate of yours would be a fool to turn you down if ever you decided to tell him how you feel.'

Paige blushed. 'I don't know. He's so into all his digital stuff, coding and science things, and video games, and tabletop stuff. I mean, I like him for it, and he's sweet. He's thoughtful. He does the dishes and puts out the garbage without me having to ask him.'

'I think you have your answer right there,' said Chad as they resumed away from the river.

Paige giggled. 'He remembers garbage day, without fail. And he . . .'

As they made their way back, Paige went on, gushing about her roommate, Evan. Chad kept encouraging her to make the first move. Before long, he and Paige had parted, and Chad was back home.

Movement in the living room as Chad made his way to the stairs alerted him to the man who was waiting for him.

James stood from the couch, looking perplexed.

Chad took the sight of him in. 'Couldn't sleep?'

James shook his head. 'You were gone a long time. You *were* at the river, yes?' Chad nodded. James walked over to him and took his hands in his. 'I wish you'd take me with you.'

Chad realised that even if James had seemed fine at first about it, he was still upset about Chad keeping this from him for so long.

'I needed to go alone, to think.'

'Think about what?' James pleaded, his grip tightening.

'Everything that's happened,' Chad replied calmly. 'It's like I've said before.' He hesitated.

'Chad? Is there something you're not telling me?' asked James, his voice trembling. He could read him so well.

There was no hiding the truth from James. 'Tonight, I went with Paige—'

'That girl?' Fear flashed on James's face. 'Are you . . . cheating on me?'

Chad shook his head – he could only imagine the vision that the fear had brought James, of Chad being intimate with someone else. He knew how powerful such sudden and impulsive fear could be, to see so vividly something you knew to be false yet unable to believe the truth for the fear is too great.

'I've told you, James, she reminds me of Mandy. Tonight she helped me realise that it's okay for me to grieve for her, even while I hate her for what she did. Mandy hurt me and I cared about her. For the first time since it all happened, I wept for Mandy's death.'

James's expression softened and he wrapped his strong arms around Chad. 'I'm sorry I doubted you.'

He sighed. 'I'm an idiot for thinking you might . . . Of course, you wouldn't! How could I think such a thing?'

'It's normal to think all sorts when fear grips us,' Chad reassured him in understanding, caressing him in turn. 'And this is something I've been keeping for myself, and now I've shared with someone else, someone who isn't my husband.'

He pulled away just enough to look James in the eyes – in his beautiful brown eyes – and convey the intensity of his love.

'But you have nothing to fear, James. I'm devoted to you and solely you. I chose the monogamous path when I got down on one knee.' James's eyes reflected chagrin and it tugged at Chad's heart. 'Paige is a stranger to what happened, and that helped. Inviting her tonight was a spontaneous last-minute thing, but that does not mean I'm hiding it from you or that I don't want to share that grief with you. I promise I will when I'm ready.'

'Okay,' replied James. 'I'm just . . . so in love with you it drives me mad sometimes and . . .' He trailed off.

'You've been spending too much time with Julian.' Chad smiled mildly, a bit sheepishly.

James breathed out a small chuckle. 'Yeah, maybe.'

Chad pulled James to him. 'Oh, baby, you know you're the only one for me – now and always – and I've got eyes only for you.'

'Only eyes?'

'My mouth, my tongue, my entire *body* is yours, James.'

James growl-chuckled, and the two hurried up the stairs, already ripping each other's clothes off.

CHAPTER NINE

A few weeks passed and they were in the heart of July. No new information had been discovered. Ian and Rayan continued to accompany James everywhere he went, though Troy had made no new appearance. It was becoming increasingly annoying to James, having to keep looking over his shoulder.

James returned from the club, it was the middle of the night. Ian and Rayan headed upstairs with whispered arguments as always. They now shared the room – there was, after all, a couch in there – but they still argued about who got to use the bed each night.

James lingered for a moment, collecting his thoughts. That's when he noticed Chad sitting in the living room, in the same spot where James usually sat when waiting up for him – he looked like he'd been waiting for him. He seemed hesitant and his heartbeat quickened.

'Hey,' Chad said softly, leaning forward. James echoed it. 'I, uh, I'm going to the river.'

James nodded, feeling a pang of disappointment. Now that Chad had opened up a bit more, he was grateful to know Chad wasn't hiding it – even if this was only the second time he had explicitly told him when he was going.

'I'd like you to come with me.'

This threw James off and his stomach did something akin to tightening. 'I'd like that.' James smiled, though he was nervous at the prospect of visiting the place Chad had kept secret from him for over a year. 'I know it's a big step for you to share this private place with me.'

Chad chewed his lip nervously. 'I'm sorry you're not the first one I bring there.'

'Paige,' voiced James. He observed Chad as the vampire went on.

'She works at the corner shop along the road to the river.'

'I remember.'

'Even while she's very different from her, she reminds me of . . .' Chad looked down, 'you know.'

James still didn't quite understand what Chad's relationship with this Paige girl was, but he knew it was just a casual friendship and nothing more, even if James had thought for a brief moment a few weeks back it could have been more.

'Please know that . . . it's not that I didn't want to bring you first, but . . . she helped me, without knowing what happened, without knowing what we are, she just . . .'

'I understand.' James walked over to Chad, who rose to his feet, and placed his hands on his face. 'I can't say I'm not disappointed or jealous, but it's not that kind of jealousy.' Chad's eyelashes fluttered as he blinked rapidly, his eyes glistening. 'Chad, baby, I just want you to let me in. I don't want you to suffer alone. Whatever you're going through, I want to be there with you.'

'Then come.'

James nodded to reiterate confirmation that he wanted to go with Chad.

Chad took James's hand and dashed them out the door to the river. While James could bound faster than most werewolves, a vampire's speed – a vampire elder's speed, on top of that – was more impressive than any James had ever witnessed. Being dashed *by* Chad was always a rush.

Before long, the two of them stood on some large rocks on the riverbed, the treeline of the small wood several feet behind them.

'This is where I've been coming to think,' said Chad.

'It's a lovely view,' remarked James. The crescent moon reflected on the water, and there were no city lights here, so he could see the stars shine brightly in the sky.

Chad held his hand tightly, looking down at the rocks. 'I want to forgive myself for not confronting her. I want to forgive myself for making her resentful.'

'Chad, baby!' James came to stand in front of him, placing his hands on his shoulders. 'You didn't "make her resentful." She already was. You did everything for her, you did everything you could. What Mandy became . . . that isn't your fault.'

'I cared about her so much – like a sister, James,' mewled Chad. 'And then she did what she did, and now she's dead. I can never have closure with her. And it grieves me that she's no longer with us. She was an important part of my life for more than two hundred years.'

Chad looked away and James gently turned his face back to him. Chad stared into James's eyes, the vampire's charcoal eyes pained with melancholy.

'I miss her and grieve for her like I grieve the death of anyone,' voiced Chad.

'And you're allowed to.' James downcast his eyes. 'I know I didn't understand at first, but just because she betrayed you and had to be killed, doesn't mean you're not allowed to mourn her death like you would anyone else's.'

He met Chad's eyes again. 'Thank you for sharing this place with me, and for trusting me with your burdened emotions.'

Chad pulled James into a tight embrace. He kissed his neck and James felt a flutter, despite the mood.

'I want to forget the torment it brings me,' Chad whispered.

James felt a pang – he knew that wouldn't solve the issue no matter how much he wanted his husband. 'You'll have to face it one day.'

'I know. One day.'

James felt his husband's lips curl up into a smile as Chad continued to graze them on his neck.

'But I do feel some liberation,' Chad continued, 'and I am ready to begin the journey of letting go.'

That reassured James.

Chad kissed James's neck again, knowing full well what James would feel from it, and James let a growl escape him. He in turn kissed Chad's neck before their lips came together, indulging in their passion and eliciting shivers of elation within each other's bodies.

* * *

Chad and James excitedly unbuttoned each other's shirts before peeling them off each other. Chad nibbled James's cheek, letting out a loud whispery breath.

Chad knew he sometimes used his desires to mask his woes, but the comfort and relief of bringing James here and having his understanding roused his primal needs.

Bending, Chad undid James's belt and pulled out his throbbing cock, still forming and still a bit soft in Chad's hand. He pulled James's boxers down just enough and licked his werewolf's testicles.

'Oh, Chad, baby,' breathed James. Chad began lapping away. 'Oh, yeah, lick those balls, baby, lick my fucking hairy balls.'

Chad engulfed a testicle in his mouth and James moaned. 'Oh, fuck, baby.'

Chad gently nudged the testicle out with his tongue and smiled up at James as he licked away. James's dick, still in Chad's unmoving hand, was hard as steel.

Chad pulled away and flared his eyes, extending his canines and baring them at James whose cock pulsed in anticipation, and he slid James's erection between his fangs. James sighed gutturally. Chad's own erection was pulsing, pushing against his pants, wanting only to be let free.

Chad sucked James, sliding his husband's cock between his teeth, and he reached down to undo his pants and pull out his erect length.

'Fuck, baby,' breathed James.

James dug extending claws into Chad's back and scratched him as he roared orgasmically. Chad grunted, the pain numbed by his mounting pleasure. The scratches healed instantly as James continued up Chad's back, creating more pain-and-pleasure pulses of adrenaline that increased Chad's arousal. Chad groaned gutturally, breathing deeply, purring for a few breaths.

'Baby, you're gonna make me melt here.'

Chad knew how James felt – weak in the legs from the pleasure pulsing through their bodies.

Chad pulled up and James gently passed his claws over Chad's chest – this time, the sensation was more tickle-and-pleasure.

Grabbing both their cocks, Chad began stroking vigorously.

'Oh, baby,' moaned James.

'Baby,' echoed Chad.

Their mouths came together as their euphoria mounted. Chad could feel the tingle from the heat in his body as James's tongue licked every inch of the inside of his mouth. Their shafts rubbed against each other. James placed a hand around Chad's hand and pumped with him.

They stroked each other hard, moving in tandem. James rubbed his thumb over Chad's shaft. It was a tickle that always turned Chad into putty in his husband's arms.

Elation rose inside of him and Chad shouted into James's mouth. James shouted immediately after and warm fluid spilled over both their hands and abdomens, streaming down their lengths as they ejaculated their orgasms together.

James tilted his head back, shouting out gruffly one final time as his cock jerked against Chad's. Chad pulsed and moaned out, his mouth agape. Then both sighed in elation.

'Fuck that felt invigorating,' Chad breathed, still feeling remnants of his orgasm rippling through his body.

James chuckled, passing his clean hand through Chad's dark, curly hair.

'Oh, there they are,' a familiar voice announced. 'Told you, nothing to—' Ian and Rayan came into view before Chad and James could react. 'Oh, fuck! Shit!' Ian turned away, shielding his eyes as the moonlight glinted on the husbands' exposed asses.

'Shit!' James cursed. 'Ian!'

'Rayan insisted!' Ian defended.

Chad quickly snatched up his shirt off the ground as James pulled up his pants. Chad used his shirt to wipe their semen off and they quickly zipped up their pants. James put his shirt back on, leaving it unbuttoned, before securing his belt and holstered gun.

Chad merely tied his shirt around his waist. 'Can't exactly put this on now, can I?'

'Don't wanna know!' Ian insisted, hand still shielding his eyes.

'You can look now, we're decent,' said James.

Ian cautiously turned back, peeking through his fingers before removing his hand from his eyes. This amused Chad.

'You both have formidable forms,' expressed Rayan, who had assumed male form.

'What, you peeked?' Ian squirmed. James chuckled. Chad merely shook his head.

'Peek would mean I was careful to steal but a small glance,' replied Rayan. 'There is no shame in admiring another's naked form.'

Ian blew out an exasperated breath. 'Anyway, you two snuck out of the house,' he complained.

'For once I have to agree with Ian,' said Rayan as Chad and James joined them up the rocks near the trees. 'You could have given us a heads-up, we would have trailed behind you at a reasonable distance.'

'Ew, no,' Ian grimaced. 'No offence, James, but my relationship with you is too platonic for me to stand guard while you're having sex just a few paces away.'

'Then are you ready to relent on being his bodyguard since I am willing to do just that?' retorted Rayan.

'Here they go again,' sighed James. Chad couldn't help but chuckle.

Ian pointed behind him as they started through the trees. 'We followed your scent. Knew you'd be around here somewhere when we saw the car parked further down.'

'I admit, I'm a little wobbly after such an intense—'

'Yeah, that's cool!' Ian interrupted, blocking his ears.

'Oh, my god, Ian, you're such a child sometimes,' laughed James. 'Why don't you bring the car around.' James handed him his car keys. 'I need to sit and catch my breath after that.'

'Same here,' breathed Chad, biting his lower lip, wanting to devour James all over again.

'Why me?' asked Ian. 'I'm your bodyguard – your *official* bodyguard.'

'And yet you fail at your job every time,' rebuked Rayan.

'Every time?' muttered Ian. 'That was *one* time.' He made a one with his index finger in Rayan's face.

Rayan casually pushed Ian's finger away from his face. 'Now be a good pup and go fetch.'

'What the hell did you just say to me?' Ian demanded, taking a step towards Rayan and getting in his space.

James chuckled. 'I kind of like that, though.' Ian turned to him, glaring. James motioned with his hand to dismiss him. 'Now be a good pup and go fetch.'

Ian opened his mouth, seething, and grinned in annoyance at James. 'Fuck you.' He turned and left. James laughed.

Chad eyed Rayan, smirking at him. 'Deny it all you want, Rayan, but you so have a thing for Ian, just as much as he has a thing for you.'

They found a park bench to sit on and James stretched out his legs, reclining as he sat down next to Chad.

'I haven't a clue what you're on about, Chad,' replied Rayan, suppressing a smile, his cheeks looking flushed.

Rayan placed his fists on his hips, taking a look around. He scowled just as Chad sensed movement nearby. James sniffed the air.

'Shit!' James hissed.

Taking his gun in hand, he bolted up. So did Chad, ready to dash, only to come face to face with Troy. Chad staggered back as he halted immediately.

'Hello again, James Sharpe.'

Rayan placed himself protectively in front of James and Chad, arms out to either side. Chad hissed at Troy, canines extending.

Troy hefted a weapon that looked like a cross between a shotgun and a crossbow. He was alone, but something told Chad his new weapon was more dangerous than his band of werewolves and vampires.

'I've brought a new toy, and I can't wait to test it on you.'

Chad grabbed James by the arm and pulled him to him as the weapon thundered – a large bullet whizzed past them. It lodged itself into a tree trunk. Chad whipped his head to stare at it. It looked just like a spearhead.

'Look out!' shouted Rayan, pushing them away from the bullet as it exploded – dozens of tiny shrapnel of silver sprayed from the shell, barely missing them.

'Fuck!' Chad stared back at Troy, his shock replaced by dread.

'Your friend's not the only one who's not afraid to use silver,' sneered Troy.

'Except he's immune to it, you're not,' retorted James.

'So what? I'm a man who's not afraid to take risks.'

Troy pulled back a lever that made a loud clicking noise. Chad dashed James away. As they made their escape, James shot at Troy, who dodged every bullet that came his way. Rayan shimmered, seeming to disappear from view as he materialised into true fae form and then back again.

'Handy trick you've got there, fae,' shouted Troy as he bounded after them, 'but I'm afraid it won't keep you alive.'

Another one of his bullets landed on the ground in front of them and they had to backtrack before they'd get sprayed with the silver shrapnel.

'This can only be Constantia's doing,' concluded Chad.

He clocked a shadow behind Troy and Ian came down on top of the enemy werewolf, jumping on him from behind, plunging a knife into him, but at the last second the rival Alpha jerked sideways and the knife plunged into his shoulder instead.

Crying out gruffly, Troy shoved Ian away from him, and plucked the knife out as the four of them ran to the car that waited in the middle of the street just beyond the treeline.

Behind them, Troy clocked his weapon again, ready to shoot another one of his special bullets.

James reached for the door handle as the weapon sounded off.

The bullet whizzed towards James's heart.

'James!' cried Ian.

The werewolf lunged in front of his Alpha and the bullet hit him square in the left shoulder. He cried out in pain. 'Argh!'

'Ian!' Rayan shrieked.

James caught Ian as he fell back. A shrill scream escaped Ian that ran Chad's blood cold. Ian clutched at his shoulder, wailing in agony and bending forward, blood gushing from the wound. James glared at Troy, murder in his eyes.

'Good luck surviving that,' snarled Troy.

'You're going to pay for this, Troy!' James seethed.

Chad jumped into the driver's seat, as James carried Ian into the back of the car. Rayan jumped in the passenger seat and James stuck his arm out, shooting at Troy who was already bounding away.

'Press on it, Chad!' James growled.

The tires screeched as Chad sped as fast as he could towards the house. Behind him, Ian screamed and shrieked. Chad untied his shirt from around his waist and tossed it to James, who tried to put pressure on the wound with it to stop the bleeding.

'Fuck, it hurts, fuck.'

'Ian, just hold on okay – we're going to get that bullet out and—'

'It's too late!' growled Ian before wailing again. 'That micro shrapnel is . . . argh, I can feel it spreading inside my body.'

James punched the back of the seat. 'You're not dying on me, Ian.'

'James . . .' Ian shook his head as he jerked and twitched. 'It burns, my whole body burns.'

'No!' cried James.

* * *

James kicked the door open as he carried Ian into the house, arms beneath him as Ian's blood spilled onto the floor. 'Liam!' he urgently yelled to be heard over his best friend's agony. 'Liam!!!' James bounded up the stairs, skipping every other step, Chad and Rayan on his heels.

'What in sane hell is going— Oh my god!' cried Rachel, who hurried up the stairs in her nightgown, avoiding the large droplets of crimson.

Ian was drenched in blood. James placed him gently on the bed in the room that had become Ian's. James sat on the bed beside Ian, holding his hand and stroking his feverish forehead. The affected area was already black with snaking tendrils spreading quickly over Ian's flesh.

'Liam!' James shrilled.

'I'm here, I'm here, what's—' His eyes widened in shock. 'What the fuck happened?'

'Nrhh, argh!' Ian rocked from side to side as he lay in bed, tears streaking down his face.

'Troy, that's what happened,' seethed James.

'A new kind of bullet,' Chad explained quickly.

Liam sat on the bed on the other side of Ian as everyone gathered in the room. He ripped open Ian's shirt and inserted his thumb and index into the bullet hole and pulled out the bullet. He scowled at it – it was but an empty shell now.

Liam turned to his sister. 'Dispose of this in a safe place, Rachel, we'll need to study it.'

'Got it. Whatever else you need, just tell me.' She left the room.

'It exploded silver into his body,' James mewled. 'Please help him. Heal him.'

Liam gently placed his hand on Ian's wound. Ian gritted his teeth before another wail escaped his lips. More tears poured from his eyes as he tightly kept them closed. Liam spat on the wound but it did not subdue the pain or change the infected area.

Rachel returned with towels and wet cloths. Julian took them from her and helped James tend to Ian. Chad placed a hand on James's – that's when James realised how much he was trembling.

Liam bent and placed his lips around the opening of Ian's wound, and his cheeks drew in, indicating he was sucking blood. After a few moments, he pulled up and spat the blood into a towel, his face crinkled – from the foul taste of the poison, no doubt. However, Liam's treatment had barely done anything to change the colour of the infected area – the tendrils of black continued to visibly spread on Ian's chest, and the werewolf continued to shake and grit his teeth in pain.

'The silver has seeped into his bloodstream,' Liam said quietly. 'It exploded inside his flesh, yes?'

More of Ian's skin was completely infected and looking like black ink was coating it as beads of black sweat formed around the area now.

'It'll soon reach his heart,' said Liam, his voice low.

James shut his eyes, a tear escaping his eye. 'This is all my fault.'

'It's Troy's fault!' Ian managed. 'I saved your life, James. I . . . nrrrh . . . bodyguard.'

'Yes, you're his bodyguard,' Rayan quavered, looking just as frightened as James felt. 'You idiot. Should have let me be the bodyguard instead.'

'Liam,' whispered James, 'is there nothing you can do to save him?'

Ian's body jerked as he began convulsing in pain. James's heart sank.

'He's dying!' James cried. 'Liam,' he pleaded, 'please! Is there something you can do – *anything?*'

'Yes, but . . . The infection is too deep in his blood now.' Liam placed his hands on Ian's shoulders. 'There is only one thing that can save you now, Ian. I can do it, and my saliva will spread throughout your body to heal you. You will be transformed, but I need your consent to—'

Before Liam could finish, Ian presented his neck and pointed at his vein, his jaw tight, unable to talk.

'So be it.'

Liam brought his canines to Ian's neck and punctured him. James saw Julian turn his face away before looking back again. Liam stayed for a long moment, drinking in Ian's blood, James guessed to ensure his saliva was truly in Ian's bloodstream.

Ian was trembling and he jerked his head back, groaning. He grabbed a hold of Liam's back with both hands. His legs jerked out as he continued to twitch.

Julian beside Chad tensed and turned his head away again.

'He's in pain,' Chad whispered.

'I know, it's just . . .'

'I know,' replied Chad.

A turning always looked more intimate to some than it was. Julian had been the one to turn Liam and they were lovers. The experience had been very intimate for them and Liam had been Julian's first turning. Ian was Liam's first turning, and even from James's angle, it looked intimate though it was not. James knew Julian was one to feel jealousy, even when he did not mean to.

James couldn't fault his friend for feeling a pang. The bond between turner and turned could be very intense at times. It was the same with werewolves, especially that the one turning another was feral at the time of turning.

Ian breathed in deeply as Liam pulled away. The werewolf's eyes shot open, flaring yellow as his claws extended. Then his eyes paled, and he gasped loudly, his canines lengthening vampirically for the first time. The infection on Ian's skin cleared up, each tendril rescinding to its point of origin until the wound closed itself up.

Ian's eyes widened and he laughed as he caught his breath. 'Wow, this feels out of this world!'

'Well, a rare kind creating another rare kind,' muttered Chad. He wiped a tear from his eye. 'You may discover some special abilities unique to only you.'

'Really?' asked Ian, colour returning to his face.

'It is said that when a *Sui Generis Lamia* turns another, they develop a rare ability none other has ever had. I'm curious what yours will be.'

Liam and James helped Ian to sit up. Julian placed a hand on Liam's shoulder. 'I'm proud of you,' he whispered.

'Thanks,' Liam whispered back. They smiled, relieved Ian was alive.

James sob-laughed. 'It worked. You're a werevamp, Ian, and you're alive! You idiot, you saved my life.' James pulled Ian into a tight embrace. 'I'll never forget this. I'll forever be grateful, my friend, my packmate. Fuck, you're like a brother to me, Ian.'

'I'm your best friend, and your bodyguard. That's what I'm here for, James.'

James's heart felt so tight – he was so grateful, so relieved, and yet so scared. 'Oh, god, Ian.' He allowed himself to weep as he held his friend for a moment more. He pulled away, wiping his eyes. 'I fucking owe you one.'

Ian shook his head. 'I'm just glad I live to see another day where I can continue to keep you safe.'

Rayan looked away, bowing his head. 'I suppose you're not as selfish as I had judged you to be.' His voice was low, and he wiped a tear from the corner of his eye.

Ian beamed at them all. 'Liam, thank you, you saved my life.'

James echoed the sentiment with a whispered, 'Liam, thank you so much.' He embraced him from the side.

'I'm glad I have this healing thing. Welcome to the world of vampires.'

Ian laughed.

'It'll take some getting used to,' Chad cautioned him. 'You should take it slow, let your body adapt.'

'So I might have a unique ability,' mused Ian. 'Am I also immune to silver now?'

'No,' Chad replied in warning. 'You are a werevamp. What you *should* be immune to, if legend is correct, is the sun. Since you were a werewolf first, it should be fine for you to walk outside in the day, but we should be cautious before—'

Ian bounced out of bed, quicky removing his blood-stained shirt and pulling on a clean one, and darted downstairs. The others hurried after him as dawn turned to morning.

'Oh my God, Ian,' shouted James, skipping the last few steps and jumping down. He was still processing all the emotions from the past few hours. 'Can you be a little less impulsive! What if the legend isn't true?'

Ian ran out to stand in the backyard, arms spread out as James stood by the door staring at him. The vampires were looking on from a safe distance.

Keisuke and Rachel stood nearby, bouncing a bumbling Hikaru who was pointing at Ian and smiling, drooling over himself.

Ian turned towards the baby. 'I'm alive. Yes, I am. Your uncle Liam saved my life. Yes, he did.'

Hikaru clapped his hands happily.

'I told you he liked you,' Keisuke expressed.

'Ian,' James insisted, chiding him, 'please be cautious. You were turned by a vampire – what if the sun harms you?'

'If the legend isn't true, we'll know soon enough, but . . .' Ian looked up at the sky. 'I think it's safe to say I'm fine.' He held out his hands and looked at his arms. 'How soon should I start feeling anything if I am to feel anything?'

'Wilbur can manage half an hour,' replied Chad, 'but his skin feels like it's sunburnt the whole time.'

'Nope, not feeling sunburnt.'

Ian grabbed a lawn chair and lounged on it, reclining and crossing his hands behind his head. He craned his neck towards the others. 'Pass me a cold one, will you? I need a good drink after all that.'

'*You?* Need a good drink?' Rayan barked. 'You are so . . .' He exhaled slowly.

Ian flicked his lighter on as he placed a cigarette on the edge of his mouth. He lit the cigarette and took a long drag. He exhaled slowly. 'This is the best fucking smoke I've had in all my life.'

'A lot of things you'll experience after coming that close to death will feel like the best in your life,' noted Liam. He winked at Julian.

'You sure it's not because you were turned?' asked Julian.

'It makes it double better.' Liam silly-giggled.

James sighed, grabbing a couple of beers from the fridge, and he stepped out, joining Ian and grabbing another lawn chair for himself. He passed his friend a beer and they clinked their cans together after popping them open.

'To lives saved,' said Ian.

'To lives saved,' echoed James, feeling a pang in his heart. He watched Ian drink from the can. 'I nearly lost you.' He shook his head and glanced back inside the house. Liam and Julian excused themselves and left the kitchen. James's eyes stayed on the baby. 'We were just a tad older than Hikaru is now when our mothers became friends and we met.' James turned back to Ian. 'I wasn't ready to lose the best friend I'd ever had.'

Ian smiled fondly at him. 'I'd do it again, you know – take a silver bullet for you.' He smiled up at the sun and closed his eyes, drawing another long pull from his cigarette and blowing out the smoke towards the sky before sipping his beer.

After a while, James felt all the energy leave his body and he needed a nap. He and Chad retreated to their bedroom for a few hours, while the others cleaned up the blood, both in the house and in the car. When they returned downstairs, Ian was still out there, sunbathing in nothing but his shorts.

'You trying to get a good tan?' asked James, crossing his arms and leaning his shoulder on the doorframe.

'You got that right,' replied Ian. An empty tall glass stood on a small outdoor table next to him. 'Did you know that blood in a fruit smoothie actually tastes good?' James shook his head, suppressing his laugh.

'Oh, Keisuke and Rachel put leftovers for you and Chad aside.'

Liam, Julian, and Rayan joined them and they ate together while Ian remained outside. The sun began to set. Ian was fine, but James still couldn't help but feel worried – he still wasn't over the shock that Ian could have died – that Ian nearly died, had it not been for Liam – that it would have been James in his place had Ian not taken that bullet for him – and that it was all his fault. He felt troubled, and Chad looked just as pensive.

'I think you can come in now, the sun's setting,' said James, his tone bored. 'I think it's safe to assume you can be out in the sun.'

'Sweet!' Ian entered the house and the group went to sit in the living room. 'But it sucks that silver can still kill me. As long as Liam's close by to heal me though, I'm good.'

'Don't get reckless,' Rayan warned, face clouded over in a frown. Liam and Julian gave Ian a look that said they agreed. Chad remained silent.

James sighed. 'If it hadn't been for me, you wouldn't have needed healing in the first place.'

'Not your fault you needed protecting,' countered Ian.

'But I'm the one Troy's after,' insisted James, his voice increasing speed with every added thought. 'Because I'm the Alpha, because of the alliance, because I agreed to it, signed for it, pushed for it.'

'It's not your fault Troy's a maniac.' Ian rested his elbows on his knees. 'It's Troy's fault.'

'He wouldn't be after me if . . . The demands he made the first two times I encountered him.' James felt his frustration mount. 'If it weren't for me and what I represent, none of this would be happening – none of the people I love would be in danger.'

'That's not true,' Ian argued. 'That Constantia chick would still be after anyone wanting an alliance, whether it had been started by our pack or not. And Adrienne's the one who signed the official papers to begin with.'

'But I'm the one who pushed for it!'

'Keisuke's the one who pushed for it first,' Julian reminded him, 'and it's not *his* fault any of this happened. The alliance is a good thing.'

'But if I weren't the Alpha, Ian wouldn't have needed to come back from Europe and he wouldn't have come close to losing his life!'

'But I'm alive, James! Let it go, okay! It's not your fault – none of this is your fault.'

'It is!' declared James. 'He was aiming at *me!* He was trying to kill *me! I'm* responsible for what happened, *I'm* responsible for why Troy is after me.'

'Oh my god, James, you're so stubborn,' shouted Ian. 'For the hundredth time: It's. Not. Your. Fault!'

'If I weren't aligned with vampires he wouldn't be after me!' James waved his hand in exasperation, his desperation and anger flaring up within him. 'It's *my* fault you got shot because it's *my* fault I'm Alpha . . .'

'It isn't your fault!' repeated Ian, talking over James, who was shouting to be heard over Ian's shouting.

'It's my fault I married a vampire!'

Chad drew in a sharp breath. The mood in the room shifted abruptly. Everyone grew quiet.

James sighed. 'That's not how I meant it, I just mean . . .'

Something on Chad's face changed and he averted his eyes. He stood without saying a word and exited the room towards the foyer.

'Chad!' James called out.

The front door slammed.

'Oh, come on!' James stood, angry with himself. He motioned towards the outside as he hurried into the hallway and saw that Chad had dashed away. 'The sun hasn't even finished setting!' He took his phone and dialled Chad's number as the others peered out and confirmed Chad was indeed gone. 'Come on, Chad, baby, pick up.' It went to voicemail. 'Baby, come on. Don't be like that. Chad, call me back.'

James hung up and stared out at the setting sun. Guilt and trepidation knotted his stomach as James felt his chest tighten. He slumped back down in a chair, and buried his head in his hands.

CHAPTER TEN

Chad went straight to the corner shop, controlling his fury as best he could. The sun was dipping low on the horizon, so he only felt a mild twinge on his skin that passed as soon as the sky darkened even a bit.

He swung the shop's door open so hard it banged on the wall and nearly fell off its hinges.

'Ooh, you don't look happy, babes. What's up?' Paige was just getting started and held a pen and notepad.

'I can't *believe* him!' Chad fumed. He began pacing to and fro. 'He just . . .' He brought his hands to his head and grabbed his hair in anger.

'Whoa, you had a fight with your guy?'

Chad bowed his head, dropping his hands. He tried to speak with more calm. 'We've been getting attacked, *he's* been getting attacked.'

'Because he's a Sharpe?'

'And a friend of his got hurt protecting him, real bad.' Chad lowered his voice to a seething whisper. 'Nearly lost his life.'

Chad balled his hands into fists and turned around as he sensed his eyes flare. He shut them to regain control before turning back to Paige.

'James feels guilty about it, but Ian is fine now. He could have died but he didn't. It's . . . a miracle. But when James apologised, Ian insisted that it's not his fault he's been getting attacked, and his reply—'

Chad seethed, clenching his jaw.

Paige placed her list down on the counter and stepped towards him. Her voice was filled with sympathy. 'What did he say, Chad?'

'He said it was his fault he married a—' He stopped himself.

Paige pressed her lips together in a straight line. 'Right.' She took her phone and after some quick tapping, pressed it to her ear. 'Kevin, I've got an emergency – Chad's helping me. Can you do the full shift?' Chad waited as Kevin gave his answer. 'Oh my god, you're a gem.' Paige made a kiss sound. 'Friendly kiss, because you're gay and all that, but a friendly kiss all the same.' She put her phone away. 'He's on his way.'

'You don't have to,' began Chad.

'I don't care how much James loves you, what he said to you was wrong. Whatever word is at the end of that sentence, it's wrong, and he shouldn't have said it. I'm taking you out tonight. We're going to have a nice bite to eat and hang out. And forget about boys.'

Chad chuckled, despite himself.

It wasn't long before Kevin arrived. As Paige changed in the office, Chad made idle chit-chat with Kevin. He learnt that the thirty-year-old shop owner had a teenage daughter with his best friend. They had been encouraged to hook up, and Kevin had experimented, partly to confirm to himself his sexuality. He had told her right after.

'She was so supportive.' Kevin smiled fondly. 'Merrill's the best. Except, a month or so after, she learnt she was pregnant.'

'That must've been a surprise for both of you,' Chad expressed, forgetting his woes for a moment.

Kevin chuckled. 'We decided, hell, fuck it, we're keeping it. Best decision of our lives.'

Kevin went on to explain that today, they lived in a bi-generational house so he could help raise his daughter. He had a great friendship with his daughter's mother, Merrill, who was still his best friend, who was now married. Kevin, while he had dated several men through-out the years, had yet to find Mister Right.

Chad's thoughts were brought back to his own Mister Right and he felt a pang, his heart aching anew.

Paige emerged, changed and ready. Thanking Kevin again for covering her shift, she and Chad hurried out of the shop, Paige leading Chad by the arm.

'We're not to talk about boys or their stupidity,' asserted Paige. She changed the subject and her tone. 'You want a good burger?'

Chad allowed himself a soft smile of appreciation. 'Sure.'

Paige brought him to a Fifties-style diner where they ate scrumptious burgers and talked about all sorts of things that were of interest to both of them – and there was no mention of James or what happened. Chad couldn't take his mind off it, though, or the guilt that he himself felt for his part in it all, but he appreciated the distraction. He just couldn't be in the house right now. He was scared it *was* his fault. If James weren't married to a vampire, let alone to Chad who betrayed Constantia, none of this would be happening to him. Chad just wanted James safe.

Paige and Chad ordered extra soft drinks to go and they stepped out of the diner, strolling aimlessly but pleasantly through the night.

Chad sighed, his heart aching.

'Oh my god, I can't believe you're thinking about him right now.' Paige's eyes bulged as she scolded him.

'Well, he *is* my husband.'

'Yeah, maybe, but he blamed marrying you for the attacks. That's not fair on you, it's not your fault!'

Chad's heart swelled, feeling grateful. Before he could answer, they came face to face with Troy and several from his pack.

'Fancy meeting you here,' smirked Troy. Chad tensed, eyes wide. Troy's eyes leeringly trailed the length of Paige's body as he spoke. 'Who's this lovely young lady with you? Someone you've got on the side?'

'Paige, get behind me.' Chad ordered in warning. Chad protectively stepped in front of her.

'Aw, don't you want to share?'

'Uh, Chad?' Paige asked from behind him.

'How's your friend?' sneered Troy. 'Did he take long to die? Did he suffer before his life was snuffed out?'

'The thing I don't get about you, Troy, is that you keep attacking James. Why not go after me?'

'Because that would be too easy, too obvious,' replied Troy. 'If I go after you alone, then that defies the purpose of setting things up so that you all hate each other and your petty alliance falls apart.'

Troy cracked his knuckles.

Chad reached his hand behind him. 'Paige, take my hand. At my command, jump into my arms.'

'Okay – I trust you.'

Chad saw Troy's hand move to his gun.

'Now!'

Chad turned, took hold of Paige – who jumped as instructed, wrapping both arms and legs around him as though to hide in his embrace – and dashed down the street and through alleyways with vampiric speed. He stopped when they were far enough that he knew the werewolves could not catch up or follow and when he could no longer hear any signs of pursuit from them.

Panting, Chad let go of Paige.

'Whoa, that was something.' The young woman let out a squealed laugh that sounded as nervous as it did exhilarated.

Chad took a few steps away from her, his back to her. 'Paige, I need to tell you the truth about me, the truth about who I am – about . . . *what* I am.' He turned to face her, mouth closed.

'Whoa, your eyes.' Paige pursed her lips in thought. 'So those weren't contacts?' she asked hesitantly. Chad let his mouth hang slightly open for her to see his eyeteeth. 'Whoa, your canines.'

'I'm a vampire.'

Paige took that in. Then grinned, squealing. 'Slay!'

Chad took that to be a good thing. 'And Troy is a werewolf. . . . Look, can we go somewhere to talk? I promise to tell you everything.'

Paige nodded. 'My apartment.'

Chad followed Paige's instructions to her place as he dashed them there. On the way, he filled her in on James being a werewolf and what James actually said. Chad explained what happened to Ian too. Paige nodded and only showed him understanding, every now and then voicing expressions he could only assume meant she accepted him as he was and was not judging what he was living through.

Her apartment was a cosy one, with two bedrooms, and a small kitchen and living room. As soon as she had shut the door, she shouted, 'I'm home.'

The shower was going and the bathroom door was closed.

As the two of them sat in the living room, Chad explained more about himself and the situation he was living, including what actually went down with Mandy, and Paige listened intently.

'It's a good thing your friend's immune to silver,' said Paige. 'But like, how awesome is that, though? You're, like, a superhero, Chad.'

The bathroom door opened and a young man emerged wearing nothing but shorts, towelling his hair. Chad deduced this was Evan. The young man lowered his arm as he became aware of Paige and Chad. His tousled, chestnut-brown hair gave him a slightly unkempt yet endearing look. A pair of rectangular glasses rested on his nose behind which his grey-blue eyes narrowed as he looked over at the pair.

Looking dejected, he averted his eyes. 'Oh,' he hesitated, 'you brought a man.'

'He's married.' Paige lifted Chad's hand to show his ring. 'Uhm . . .' She chewed her lip nervously.

Chad looked from Paige to Evan, retreating his hand. 'I think the two of you should admit to each other how you feel.' Both of them blushed. 'You never know what life will throw your way to try to pull you apart. Enjoy your happiness while you can and hold onto each other before the other is lost to you.'

Paige and Evan stared at each other, nervousness mixed with hope.

Chad excused himself to the bathroom. He splashed some water on his face and took a few deep breaths. Every time that persistent pang hit him, his heart clamoured. The water and breathing seemed to help.

When he emerged from the bathroom, he received a text from Paige. *Talk in the morning, you can use my bed. We'll try to be quiet.* Chad chuckled slightly.

He scrolled through his dozen unread messages, all of them from James who was fretting about him, apologising. The last one reading: *Baby, I take it back. I'm sorry. Just please come home.*

'But it's true, James,' Chad whispered to himself. 'You can't take it back . . . because . . . you're right. Part of the problem is because you married a vampire – a vampire who proposed to you – and if I weren't in the picture, your life would not be in danger.'

Chad lay down on the bed in Paige's very pink and girlie room, staring at his phone, unable to find the courage to reply.

* * *

James woke with a start. He'd slept in his clothes, holding his phone, which was now on his chest. He checked to see if Chad had replied. No such luck.

The sun was shining brightly outside. James dragged himself out of bed and went downstairs. He sent Chad another text message, hoping he would answer him.

Please, baby, just tell me that you're safe. I just need to know you're safe.

'No answer?' asked Keisuke, bringing James a steaming mug of coffee.

'Thanks, and no.' James took the mug and sipped the hot drink. It burned his oesophagus. James winced.

'At least blow on it,' Keisuke chided him. He took a sip of his own coffee.

'No Hikaru?'

'Just put him down,' replied Keisuke.

James looked around. 'It's quiet.'

'I sent Ian and Rayan out for some errands – baby supplies. It'll take them a while to find everything.'

James eyed his friend and arched a brow. 'You have a wicked sense of humour, you know that?'

Keisuke chuckled. 'Someone needs to give those two a nudge.'

James sat down in the living room, staring down at his coffee, unable to stop himself from checking his phone.

'He'll call when he's ready,' Keisuke said gently.

'I just need to know he's safe,' wept James. 'What if he ran into Troy? What if something happened and he's dead?'

'You're James Sharpe, you practically own this city,' Keisuke argued. 'If anything happens to Chad, someone will contact you. Just, try not to worry. I know it's tough, but . . .'

'I take it back.' James passed a hand through his hair. 'What I said was cruel.'

'There may have been a better way to express what you intended to convey,' began Keisuke, 'but you're not wrong.'

'But it doesn't mean I regret marrying him or that suddenly I don't love him anymore!'

'And he knows that.'

James heard two arguing voices grow louder as they approached the entrance.

'Ah, there they are now,' said Keisuke as he stood from his seat.

'I can't believe you told the clerk we were a couple!' Rayan shrilled, voice indicating the fae was in female form.

'She assumed!' argued Ian. 'I only went along with it.'

'You had an entire backstory!'

'Yes! Ever done roleplay or gone undercover? Allows you to think fast on your feet and come up with backstories on the fly.'

The door unlocked and the two barged in.

'Quietly, please,' Keisuke walked over to divest them of their shopping and bring it into the baby's room.

'You are so cocky sometimes, Ian, you're such an idiot!' Rayan complained at Ian's back.

Ian spun around, pointing a finger in Rayan's face. '*I'm* cocky? And what about you, huh? Insulting my skills as a bodyguard, insulting me every chance you get, everywhere we go, calling me pup?! I'm not a pup. I'm a werewolf – and my Alpha's bodyguard. There is honour in that, more than me just joking that I'm his best friend.'

'You weren't even there for his wedding,' retorted Rayan.

'That's between me and him,' Ian whispered harshly.

'It *is* between him and me,' James confirmed, setting his coffee down and walking to the two as they settled in. They followed James to the living room, continuing their argument.

'You claim there is honour as an Alpha's bodyguard, but what have you done as his bodyguard? You smoke, you flirt—'

'With you!' Ian pointed out.

'*Estúpido!* You are distracted, so much that you failed to protect him when Liam had to step in.'

'We pinned Troy down as a group, so that counts as me protecting James.'

'And then your foolish sense of pride sends you on the edge of death!'

'Foolish sense of pride – what the fuck?' Ian narrowed his eyes. 'It isn't pride that saved my best friend's life.' Ian's face crinkled in disdain. 'I risked my life for him. I saved his life. And what do you do? Insult me again,' he began to rant faster, 'as though I should have died for me to be worthy of respect in your eyes. I don't need this. I don't need to be undermined and disrespected at every turn by a fae who thinks they're better just because they're fae.'

'That's not what this is!' insisted Rayan.

'Then what is it, Rayan? Because from where I'm standing, you're putting me down. All you do is berate me. How do you think that makes me feel, huh?'

Rayan fell silent for a moment. Her hair and the rim of her fedora hid her face as she bowed her head. 'You *are* worthy of respect, Ian,' she said gently. 'I'm sorry if I ever made you feel otherwise.'

'Yeah, yeah, sorry my ass. In a few minutes, you're gonna start all over again.' Ian passed a hand over the top of his braids, turning around.

'Ian, please – I'm trying to apologise.' Rayan took a step forward. 'I didn't realise how much my words had affected you. I was . . . I didn't realise I hurt you.'

'Hurt me?' Ian whirled back around. 'You think you're capable of hurting me? Piss me off, that's what you do. All the fucking damn time, every day. You've shown no respect towards me since day one.'

'That's not true!' insisted Rayan.

'Hey, come on now,' James cautioned, trying to diffuse the situation. 'You were both teasing each other and it got personal. Now that it's all out in the open, you can reconcile your grievances, yes?'

'No chance.' Ian folded his arms, fuming. 'Rayan's made it clear I'm not worthy of respect, no matter what I do. Well get this, Rayan – I'm not trying to win your respect. I don't care what you think of me. I'm here for James, and I saved his life. And I'd do so again in a heartbeat. Next time, *I might die,* and then maybe, just maybe, you'll think kindly of me.'

Rayan slapped Ian across the face, seething at him. Ian gawped back in shock. The tension between the two was palpable as they continued to stare daggers at each other. James himself was taken aback.

'What the fuck?' Ian breathed after a few beats.

'You always think about yourself – you, you, you – without any second's thought to how it might make anyone else feel.'

Ian stepped up to Rayan. 'What are you trying to prove, then? Come on, let it out. Wouldn't be the first time you insulted me. Come on, come at me.' Ian took a menacing step forward, Rayan didn't budge. They glared down each other's noses.

'You're always boasting about what you did, your heroics, and you don't care how those heroics affect other people or how your attitude affects other people. You're *selfish.*'

'So? Sue me.' Ian shoved Rayan's shoulder in a taunting manner. Rayan shoved back in the same manner. 'You still haven't told me if you respect me, even with all I've done.'

'There you go again. And you still haven't apologised, even after *I* have!'

'Oh, *I*—' Ian pointed at himself – 'have to apologise, now? Fine, then, I'm so sorry.' Ian sounded annoyed, and James was wondering whether he should physically butt in or not.

'Oh, because that sounded genuine,' Rayan retorted sarcastically. 'You know, maybe next time you *should* get yourself killed. Because then I won't have to put up with your incessant cockiness twenty-four-seven!'

'That's it!' Ian shoved Rayan against the wall. She grabbed his arm and pulled back, twisting him around.

The two grappled each other to the ground – Ian flipped Rayan who kicked him, landing on top of him.

'Stop it, both of you,' James interjected. He placed a hand on each of them, but both of them kicked out. James backed away.

Ian pushed Rayan off him and jumped up into a crouch before rising. Rayan took a swing at Ian's face. His hand blocked her fist – she pushed harder and sent him staggering back. Rayan kicked her leg high and Ian had to duck. Rayan readied a quick burst of a spell and Ian hissed as it sizzled past his head.

'That all you've got, pup? Because that's what you are, just a pup who can't stop himself from repeating his few little exploits to pretend he's worth something.'

'My life *is* worth something!' Ian growled. He kicked Rayan who grabbed his leg and pulled. Ian placed his hands out to cushion his fall and followed through with a backflip.

'Should have heard yourself wailing like a baby!'

Ian's face contorted in rage. 'You want silver shrapnel to explode inside your body, huh? You'd wail in pain too.'

'You should have let *me* protect James!'

'And let *you* take all the credit? No chance.'

Glowering, the two took a step away from each other, shoulders hunched. James came to stand between them, his arms out. Ian shoved James away so hard, the Alpha staggered back and bumped into the wall.

Rayan came at Ian again. They locked arms, grabbing the other's shoulders, and shoved against each other, staggering forward and back as each of them pushed harder against the other.

'You were impulsive!' Rayan accused.

'I did what was necessary!'

Keisuke emerged from the hall and marched up to them, leaning forward on his front leg. 'That's enough!' His voice was a half-whisper, but he said it with such authority it stilled their fight. 'Settle down, you two – I just put the baby to sleep.'

Rayan seethed at Ian. 'You could have died.'

'Yeah, I bet you would've loved that,' Ian growled in response.

'No!'

Jaws tight, the two stared at each other, still pushing against the other's shoulders, but this time, the glint in their eyes was more intense than before.

Ian lunged forward, pulling Rayan to him, and their lips locked as their arms enveloped their bodies, hands already roaming madly and grappling at their clothes.

'Okay,' Keisuke lifted his arms in defeat, 'I'm going to be in the kitchen if anyone needs me.' Keisuke left the room.

James gaped as Rayan and Ian moved to the stairs, already undressing each other. He shook his head and joined Keisuke in the kitchen. 'At least *some* people's romantic lives are going well.' He pulled a chair out and slumped down at the table across from Keisuke.

'Hey, he'll come home,' Keisuke reassured.

'Yeah, but when?'

'He knows you love him.'

'I just wish it hadn't come out the way it did, you know? I feel like such an idiot.'

'He knows this. He knows you, James. Chad loves you. He probably needs to cool off somewhere. I'm certain that he'll realise—'

Something knocked into the wall upstairs – hard – the sound of glass shattering followed. Keisuke and James stared at each other, wide-eyed, waiting for the inevitable. And then the baby began to cry.

Keisuke sighed, closing his eyes and bowing his head. He placed his hands on the table and leaned his head on them.

'I'll go,' said James.

'Thank you,' sighed Keisuke.

James stood and went to soothe the baby to sleep – Hikaru would provide a much-needed distraction. He took him in his arms and sat down on a rocking chair. He watched Hikaru's face as his tears streamed down his little temples. His little baby hands reached towards James.

James gently rocked Hikaru from side to side, bouncing him and whispering reassurance to him, but Hikaru only stretched his arm out to James, crying harder.

His heart heavy with his own chagrin, James finally let his tears flow. He heaved as a faint sob escaped him.

Hikaru touched his wet cheek, calming and looking surprised. And then Hikaru reached forward and wrapped his tiny little arms around James's large chest – it was Hikaru's turn to comfort James.

James closed his eyes, pained, and exhaled shakily. Then, the two of them calmed and the only sounds that remained were the creaking of the rocking chair and their tranquil breathing.

Chapter Eleven

James observed Rayan and Ian as they sat before a scowling Keisuke – both bodyguards looked sheepish. The Japanese man, while stern, was poised, he did not raise his voice once, but his tone was authoritative. James felt this man could command armies if he wanted to.

Rayan had switched to male form and was wearing the violet fedora that complemented his usual outfit rather well, whichever form he was in when he wore it. Ian wore his shirt unbuttoned, revealing the subtle line of chest hair that ran from his pecs all the way down into his pants. Their knees touched and James noted the suppressed smiles as Keisuke finished scolding them.

'We're sorry we woke Hikaru after you put him to sleep,' Ian muttered.

'And we'll do poopy duty for the next week to make amends,' declared Rayan.

'And we promise not to make noise that'll wake Hikaru up,' Ian added.

'Good. Thank you.' Looking satisfied, Keisuke stood and left the parlour – the room was more removed from other common areas and provided a more quiet and relaxed atmosphere if not ominous in the dimness with the sun blocked out.

Rayan and Ian immediately started giggling and playfully poking each.

'I'm glad you two figured things out,' expressed James.

'We're still figuring things out, I suppose,' admitted Ian. He leaned forward, touching his nose to Rayan's. 'I reckon I still have some apologising to do.'

'Oh, I suppose I have some more apologising to do as well.' They nibbled each other's lips, rumbling soft growls as they did.

'Yes, well,' began James, 'I need to leave the house, and I'd appreciate it if my two bodyguards accompanied me.'

'Right on,' declared Ian, pulling away from Rayan.

The three made their way to the lobby where they saw Rachel arrive from work. Had the entire day gone by already? James greeted her before Ian and Rayan's conversation rose to his ears.

'I know you don't have them,' said Ian. 'But *why* don't fae have pubes?'

Rachel froze. 'Okay bye.' She turned around to start down the hall. Ian and Rayan burst out laughing.

'Don't mind them,' said James.

'I just want to know how you have head hair but nothing down there!'

'We just don't!' insisted Rayan.

Rachel stopped, swishing her hair back with her hand as she turned to the group. 'When you're done discussing . . . rugs and curtains, there are chores that need doing.'

'We'll do you one better,' said James. He beckoned the two new lovebirds and bade Rachel a good evening.

Ian and Rayan followed James to the door; he turned back to them. 'Listen, I really am happy for you, and just because my love life's in shambles right now, I don't want you to feel you have to hold back your affections on my account.'

'Don't encourage him,' muttered Rayan, smiling cheekily, 'Ian won't be able to stop himself.' Rayan turned to Ian. 'He's got no self-control.'

'And yet you're the one who keeps pouncing me.' Ian made a mock bite gnash.

'And like an obedient little pup,' Rayan purred, 'you oblige.'

'Hmmmm,' Ian growled low in his throat. 'Rawr.' He followed with a barking sound.

'Just as long as you don't do *that* the next time *I* insult you or call you pup,' James chuckled. They all laughed. James appreciated the pair and the distraction they provided.

'So where are we going, my dear Alpha?' inquired Ian as they all climbed into the car – it still smelt too much of cleaning products for James's liking.

'You'll see.' James drove them to the corner shop that stood along the avenue to the river and parked at just an angle from it across the street. Ian was in the passenger seat and Rayan was in the back behind Ian.

'What's in that shop? We staking out the place?' asked Ian. Rayan positioned himself in the centre of the backseat.

'Paige works here, she's . . . Chad's new friend,' replied James.

'Oh my god, are you stalking her?'

'We're just going to wait until she arrives at work and ask her if she knows where Chad is.'

'You are so stalking her!' Ian accused. He pointed a finger at James. 'We're not following her home.'

'No, we're not. I just . . . I just need to know Chad's safe.'

'Okay. I get it.'

The truth was that James was unable to contain his fear, so he went to the place he thought he might find Chad – or at least some answers. Ian and Rayan remained mostly quiet as the three sat in the car waiting for nightfall. Then a young woman pranced up to and into the shop.

Heart pounding in anticipation, James got out of the car and followed the young woman into the shop – he recognised her from the club a few months back. 'Hey, are you Paige?'

'Depends who's asking,' she said with a smile. Her eyes scanned his broad body before she made a face akin to recognition, her eyes widening for a moment, and then her demeanour changed.

'James Sharpe. I, uh . . .'

'Yeah, I know you. We met at the club.' Her face and tone gave away that she knew a lot more than she was letting on.

James hesitated. 'Have you seen Chad?'

'Maybe I have, maybe I haven't,' Paige replied carefully. She folded her arms, shifting her weight to one leg.

'Now I definitely know you have. Look, I'm losing my mind here, he hasn't been returning my calls and—'

'Can you blame him?!' She placed a fist on her hip. 'What you said to him was downright hurtful.'

James observed her carefully. He didn't know how much she knew, but . . . 'So Chad told you about our quarrel.'

Paige merely crossed her arms again, giving James a stern look. James was a werewolf Alpha, and here was this twenty-year-old girl staring him down and actually making him feel small in comparison, even if he was taller and broader than her. James shrank under her gaze, knowing how right she was.

Paige's expression softened and she opened her mouth to speak just as a group of young men in their late teens walked in, stealing her attention away from James.

'Oh my god, Dean! I can't believe you're still trying to come here when you know you can't. Leave.'

'I want to talk, that's all!' insisted the lad.

James recognised a pack member among this Dean's group of friends.

'Uh, Dean,' the pack member muttered, 'that's James Sharpe, the guy I was telling you about before.'

'Yeah, and?' shrugged Dean.

'You don't want to mess with him,' the pup mumbled.

'Fine, whatever!' Dean turned to Paige. 'You have to start dating guys your own age.'

'Why, you think I'm too young for the likes of James Sharpe or his husband?' retorted Paige. 'I already have a boyfriend, Dean. His name is Evan.'

'What, you're actually dating that nerd?'

James crossed his arms, flexing his muscles so they'd bulge from under his t-shirt, and stared down the group of young men.

'Is there a problem, lads?' They fell quiet. 'This young lady has asked you to leave. I suggest you run along now. Or do I have to station my people at this shop – *armed* people – as bodyguards to ensure you lads don't return?' To emphasise the threat, James placed a hand on his holster.

That got a reaction out of Dean and his eyes darted to James's hip. Realising the grave he was digging himself into, Dean and his friends began out the door.

James grabbed the pup by the collar, pulling him back into the shop and whispered harshly. 'Not so fast, pup. What the hell are you doing hanging around with the likes of a bully like that? You're never going to amount to anything if you follow his example. Come on, you're better than that.'

'Sorry, James.'

'It's not me who's going to be sorry if you can't protect your pack,' seethed James. He released the lad and watched him join his friends.

'You called him "pup".' James realised Paige was standing right behind him. He spun around. She continued. 'Is he a werewolf too?'

James's eyes widened.

'Chad told me – not like he had a choice. We ran into that . . . Troy guy, and then dashed away, so he told me who he and you are.'

James swallowed, fear gripping him. 'You ran into Troy?' The memory of Ian bleeding out in James's arms flashed through his mind. An intrusive thought of Chad suffering the same, inky silver poison spreading all over him, had James unable to see the shop he stood in. He blinked. 'Is he okay – tell me Chad's okay!' James pleaded.

'Oh, I know how it is. Not, are you okay, Paige? Were you afraid, Paige?' She shook her head in a dismissive gesture. 'Look, he's fine. He's staying at my place. He just needs time, okay?'

James felt his brows furrow as sorrow threatened to spill from his eyes. 'Please, tell him how sorry I am.'

'I'm sure he knows by the amount of messages you've sent him,' replied Paige, her tone softer now. She placed a hand on James's arm and it was somewhat comforting. 'Chad knows you love him, and he's mad about you. I can tell him he should go home, but I can't force him if he's not ready.'

James hung his head. 'I understand. Thank you.'

With nothing left to be said between the two, James backed away and exited the shop.

He got back to the car, yanking the door open, and slumped down in the driver's seat. He sighed. He looked back at the shop, yearning for Chad.

'We are *not* waiting to follow her home,' Ian reminded him.

'I just don't understand; he's ghosting me!'

'He's not ghosting you, James,' Ian reassured. James wanted to believe him. 'Chad just needs his space right now, to process everything. *You* could have been the one shot the other night, and he might feel responsible after what you said.'

'I wish I hadn't said it. If I had just expressed myself better . . .' James clamped his mouth with his fist as his sorrow threatened to spill over.

'But you did say it,' Ian said gently, 'and it hurt him.'

James brought his hand to his eyes and began to weep. 'I just miss him so much. I need my husband home with me.'

Ian gently rubbed James's back. 'He'll come home when he's ready.'

'Ian's right,' said Rayan. 'But you need to stop torturing yourself over it. Chad loves you, he might just need to sort things out before he's ready to come home. Love is complicated at times.'

'And you need to stop sending him messages like an obsessed spouse,' Ian chided, though there was kindness in his tone.

'I *am* an obsessed spouse.' James hit the steering wheel.

'Well, at least you're self-aware,' muttered Ian.

James let out a mirthless laugh.

'Come on,' Ian urged gently, 'let's go home.'

His heart heavy and fearing his marriage was already falling apart so soon after the wedding, James drove back home and returned to his empty bed where he held Chad's pillow in his arms and wept in utter despair.

* * *

Chad was gone for nearly a week. James had sent him countless messages, both voice and text. It was tempting to respond, but Chad held firm in his belief as to what now was the best course of action. Nothing would deter him from his decision.

He arrived home before James had. He stood facing the window where the pitch darkness of night threatened to squeeze his lungs.

Chad heard the door downstairs. Heavy steps on the stairs. James bid Ian and Rayan good night as the bodyguards entered their room. Reflected in the window, Chad saw James enter the room and turn on the light.

Eyes wide, James let out a few shaking breaths. 'Chad,' he exhaled. 'You're back.'

James shut the door behind him and took several steps towards Chad. The reflection showed Chad all of the emotions on James's face, and it twisted the invisible knife Chad felt in his heart.

'Baby . . .' James hesitated.

His heart heavy, holding himself firmly to quell his trembling, Chad spoke in a monotone. 'I think it's best we stop seeing each other, James.'

James drew in a sharp breath. 'What are you talking about?' he demanded.

'I've come to realise that . . .' Chad paused, not wanting his voice to crack. 'I was infatuated with the rebellious idea of a vampire and a werewolf together . . . but the truth is, I've only ever loved other vampires.'

James took a step forward and, reflected in the window, Chad could see the stern disdain on his face. 'I won't let you throw away what we have, Chad. I'm sorry I said what I said. It was wrong, that's not how I meant it. But whatever Troy throws my way, we can get through it . . . *together!*'

Chad swallowed, his throat so dry it stung. James could probably hear his racing heart beating so hard. Chad bowed his head and closed his eyes before looking back at James's reflection – he could not bring himself to turn around and face him.

'James . . . I don't want to.'

James gaped at him for several silent moments. 'What happened to "Whatever happens, it happens to us together." Huh?'

Chad's breath began to tremble. To compensate, he responded in a flat tone through clenched teeth. 'Marrying you was a mistake.' The moment he said it he felt as though a knife had pierced his heart, and the look on James's face told him he'd felt that too.

James's hands curled into fists and his face contorted in anger. 'That's low,' he seethed. 'How could you say that! *Why*— would you say that?'

'I've fallen out of love with you,' Chad blurted.

James shut his eyes tightly, turning his head to the side. 'I can't believe this,' he muttered. 'Did I *ever* mean anything to you?'

Chad steeled himself. 'No.'

There was a heavy silence. James's whisper was dangerous. 'If that's how you want it.'

James ripped his ring off his finger and hurled it at Chad so hard, Chad nearly winced. It clanked against the window before falling to Chad's feet.

James took a beat, then whirled and stormed out of the room, swinging the door open without bothering to close it and pounding down the stairs. He slammed the outside door so hard, the house shook.

Chad brought his hand to his face, shielding his eyes as tears poured down his face. He heaved and sobbed uncontrollably, collapsing to the ground. He reached for James's ring. He clutched it and brought it to his bosom.

The screech of tires told Chad James had driven off.

Chad felt like he had reached into his chest, wrenched his heart out and ripped it in two. It was a pain beyond any he had known – it hurt so much that he felt it physically. He clutched at his heart, gripping the ring in his hand. Unable to keep his sobs quiet, he heaved deeply, regretting immediately what he'd done, the lies he'd told, but he wanted to protect James, and he could not think of any other way than to separate from him.

Chad would leave town, leave the friends he had come to consider family, all to protect James – to save his life – for Chad loved him that much. He loved him so much he would die for him if it meant James would live.

Chad heaved heavily, sobbing loudly into the night, hand on the wall, the other still holding the ring at his heart, his vision a complete blur as a puddle of tears formed on the floor. It was difficult to breathe – every breath was a loud ragged wail, every exhale a tormented sob that twisted evermore the pain in Chad's heart.

Rachel appeared in the doorway with a crying Hikaru in her arms, trying to soothe him. 'Oh my god, Chad, what happened? Are you okay?' She hurried to his side while rocking the baby.

Chad stared up at her and her eyes landed on the ring in his hand. 'Oh, Chad,' she sighed in sympathy. She sat down next to him and put an arm around his shoulders, letting his nestle in the shelter of her bosom. Chad wailed in her arms, letting her rock him, and she soothed him with her whispers and gentle caresses on his hair. Chad's crying calmed but barely, as did Hikaru's – Chad continued to weep quietly in Rachel's arms.

Liam and Julian appeared in the doorway. 'What's going on?' demanded Liam, concern in his voice. They stopped when they saw Chad.

'Chad, you're back!' exclaimed Julian.

'Liam,' ordered Rachel, 'emergency comfort brew – now.'

'On it.' Liam left and hurried down the stairs.

Chad realised Keisuke had entered the room and was taking Hikaru from Rachel. Ian and Rayan were also in the room. No one said a word, they only looked on with sadness in their eyes.

Julian helped Chad to his feet, but Chad felt like he would collapse again as the weight of his sorrow bore down heavily on him, so he leaned on Julian for support.

Ian had his phone up to his ear. 'Come on, come on, pick up, man.' Ian exhaled angrily. 'James, get your ass back here or I'm coming after you myself.' He hung up and called again, fidgeting as it rang. 'Fuck!' He pulled his phone away from his ear. 'Son of a bitch! Doesn't he know it's dangerous out there alone?'

Ian looked at Rayan, the worry was apparent on the werevamp's face. Rayan, who had assumed male form, nodded, a determined look on his face.

'Rayan and I will search for James at all the safehouses we know,' asserted Ian, 'both werewolf and vampire ones – we'll call Wilbur and Adrienne, and everyone we know.'

Chad merely wept as he was led downstairs and into the living room, his entire body heavy and heaving, barely aware that Ian and Rayan had now dashed out the door.

Julian sat down next to him, an arm still around Chad's trembling shoulders. Liam brought him a hot tisane.

'Chad, look,' began Liam, crouching before him, 'I don't know what happened, but this is just a blip, okay? He doesn't mean it – he loves you and he's mad about you. He doesn't regret marrying a vampire.'

'It's not what he said the other day,' sobbed Chad, 'it's what I said tonight!' Chad heaved, taking in a lungful of air – he was crying so hard, he was beginning to hyperventilate. 'As long as we're together, he's in danger. I love him. I want to protect him, but we're from two different worlds – vampires and werewolves aren't supposed to mix. So to protect him, I— I told him . . .' He couldn't finish his sentence. Instead, he began to heave loudly again.

'Oh no, Chad,' sighed Julian, 'you haven't gone and done that?'

'I just want him safe,' Chad sobbed, clutching James's ring even more and bringing it to his lips, as though holding it in a prolonged kiss would bring James back.

Rachel walked to Chad and slapped his arm with the back of her hand.

'What the hell, Rachel!' snapped Liam, rising. 'Can't you see—'

'He needs to snap out of it,' asserted Rachel. She looked down at Chad, her eyes telling him she was deeply troubled. 'I'm sorry, Chad, but you're an idiot. Do you actually think this is going to protect him? The damage is done – all you're doing is hurting the two of you. You love each other, for heaven's sake!'

'She's right,' said Keisuke, entering the room while rocking the baby. 'What James needs is *you* – not to be safe *without* you, but for you to figure it out *together*. I watched you claim your vows to each other last winter on your wedding night. Now ask yourself this: Would an honourable man back out on those vows so readily? Or would a coward?'

'I think the two of you need to work on your pep talk skills,' Chad muttered. Yet somehow, already, it was working.

'We're trying to talk some sense into you, Chad,' insisted Rachel, her voice softer now. 'Sometimes tough love is what's needed.'

'So you love me?' Chad teased, looking up at her, trying to forget his pain.

Hikaru murmured.

'What's that? You want Chad to go find James and reconcile?' Keisuke asked the baby.

Hikaru smiled. 'Gah!'

'You hear that, Chad? Even Hikaru agrees with us.'

Chad looked at the baby's smiling face, and tears welled in his eyes once more. Julian took the hot cup of tea from him and Chad brought his hands to his face, bending forward and weeping. As Liam sat down beside Chad, both he and Julian rubbed his back gently for a while until Chad calmed again.

The group sat together in silence, drinking the tea. Eventually, they all dozed off before being awoken several hours later by the sound of the front door.

'James?' Chad sat upright.

'Sorry,' voiced Rayan. He wore a look of sympathy. 'We haven't found him.'

'No one's seen or heard from him,' complained Ian. 'He's gone AWOL!'

Chad's heart sank.

Then suddenly, his eyes widened as a memory played in his mind. 'I know where he is.' And like being doused with cold water, his mind was jolted to a clear state – he knew what he had to do.

Chad stood and bolted to the door. He paused briefly and looked back at everyone. 'Thank you, for making me realise the mistake I've made. No matter how much I regretted it or didn't want it, I was convinced it was for the best. Now I know how wrong I was, and I'm going to fix this – I'm going to win back my husband.'

With that, Chad was out the door, dashing with vampiric speed.

Chapter Twelve

James paced like a prowling wolf in the basement room where he was staying, shoulders hunched and hands balled into fists. If he had the ability to turn feral at will, he would be pacing on all fours. He needed to unleash his pent up anger. He stopped and slammed a fist into the wall, perforating it. He screamed, his voice rough.

'How could you do this,' he shouted into the void. 'How could you do this to us!' He pressed his thumbs on his eyes, but tears still flowed. 'Idiot!'

The doorbell rang a fancy tune and there came an urgent rap at the door. James's heart skipped a beat. But it couldn't be!

'He's downstairs,' Olivia voiced.

James held his breath. From the entrance of the room, James watched the stairs in earnest as someone hurried down them . . . And then *he* came into view, tears streaming down his face.

'You found me,' James whispered.

'I remembered the town, the picture of the house . . . I followed your scent.'

James stared at Chad in disbelief, wanting at once to punch him and pull him into his arms. Chad took several cautious steps towards James.

'I can't do it!' the vampire wept, shaking his head. 'I thought I was strong enough but I'm not.'

James merely stared at Chad.

'I wanted to—' Chad's tone grew pleading. 'James, everything I said back there, it's not true, it was all a lie. I thought that by breaking up with you, I would be protecting you, but it's barely been a night and I can't bear to be away from you. Please forgive me, James. I love you, I—'

'You idiot!' James breathed. 'I know.' Chad gaped at him. 'I know that's what you were doing.' James sighed, bowing his head. 'I was too angry to tell you then – you were so determined to tell me those hurtful lies, I couldn't stand to be in the same room as you anymore.'

James met his husband's gaze, feeling the fire in his eyes as they flared. 'Do you think I would let the man I love go so easily without fighting for him? Do you think I would give up on our love just because there are those who are trying to eliminate me? You are an idiot if you think that.'

'Then I am an idiot for not realising that your love for me is as strong as mine is for you.'

James grabbed Chad by the arm, pulling him close and wrapped his strong arms around him tightly – Chad was so warm, it felt comforting just to hold him again. Chad heaved and James felt his husband's hot tears in the nape of his neck. James shut his eyes tight and his own tears wet Chad's shirt.

A muffled sob escaped Chad and his warm breath caressed James in ways that made his heart hurt from the whirlwind they'd been through.

'We hurt each other,' James whispered. 'I'm sorry I said . . .' He pressed his lips together.

'You were right,' said Chad, 'and I understand how you meant it.' The vampire's grip tightened and James pressed his cheek against Chad's.

Both of them wept for a few moments before James growled angrily, pushing Chad against the wall and pinning him there.

'Don't ever hurt me like that again! You hear me?'

Chad's brows furrowed in chagrin. 'Your life is in danger because of me.'

James shook his head, clenching his jaw. 'Don't you get it? I'd rather *die* than live without you!'

A sob escaped Chad's lips as he grabbed James's face and pressed his lips against his. James felt his passion throughout his entire body, and it felt so good to taste his husband again after all those days without him.

Chad pulled away. 'I promise!' Chad knelt on one knee, looking up at James's face, and holding up the ring James had thrown at him – *his* ring. 'I shall ask my husband to stay married to me.' Chad's voice echoed James's sobs. 'I promise to never retract my promises to you ever again.' James felt like his heart was going to explode with the love he felt.

'James, baby . . .' Chad blinked a few times. 'James Sharpe, my husband, my Alpha . . .' Sweet longing pulled at James's heart, and he exhaled, elated and moved. 'Will you take me back?'

'I was always yours, Chad, and I always will be. I love you so much it drives me crazy.' James stared down at Chad. 'I accept – you know I do. So, yes, yes I *will* take you back, my husband, my Partner-Alpha.' His husband slipped the ring back on James's finger – somehow, James felt whole again.

'Whatever else I can do to prove to you . . . whatever else I can offer you . . .' Chad continued to look up at James in earnest.

James found himself smirking, despite the tears. 'There *is* something you can offer me, baby.'

Chad's eyes flared, and James knew Chad knew exactly what he meant. James's body reacted with pulses inside his groin and stomach, making his anticipation and desire mount.

Chad's hands lunged at James's belt and whipped it off him. The belt's buckle clattered against the wall as Chad plunged a hand into James's pants. James breathed out, his growl low and throaty, as his husband's warm hands wrapped around his hardening cock.

James pushed the door closed just as his length was swallowed by Chad, sliding deep into his throat. James tilted his head back.

'Fuck, that feels good!'

Chad slid his mouth to his shaft and then back down again, James bucked forward. It felt so good, but more than anything, James wanted to taste his husband. He wanted to devour him.

'Fuck, it's been so long, Chad.'

James grabbed Chad's arms and pulled him up, waiting no more than a beat before he captured his lips in a searing kiss. He opened his mouth and thrust his tongue onto Chad's mouth, feeling the vampire's canines just as they were extending.

James barely pulled away, breathing heavily as a sob escaped him. More tears twinkled in Chad's eyes too.

'Oh, Chad, baby, what are we like?'

Chad offered him a wan smile. 'We're a vampire and a werewolf navigating uncharted waters.'

James grinned through his tears and growled, 'Then that makes us trailblazers!'

He tugged at Chad's shirt, fumbling with his buttons and tripping over his falling pants as they frantically ripped each other's clothes off. James landed on the couch that sat at the foot of the bed and leaned his head back as Chad got on top of him, straddling him.

Devouring each other's lips, they finished undressing hurriedly, eagerly.

'I want you so fucking bad right now,' James whispered huskily. He placed his hands on Chad's bare chest, the vampire's sleek taupe and hairless chest already hot and sticky.

Chad jumped up to remove his pants and landed back on top of James, his hard cock pulsating onto James. James pulled Chad closer to him, to feel his naked body against his. He breathed in deeply, intoxicated by Chad's musky scent.

Chad grabbed his dick and slapped it against James's. 'Oh, yeah.'

Chad slid himself down until his mouth was aligned with James's erection and he licked his balls. Chad lapped away quickly, rubbing his thumb over James's oozing shaft, just like he knew James liked it.

James felt sweat bead on his chest, the A.C. in the house no longer taking effect as the pleasure mounted in his body, making his chest hair stick to his tawny skin. Tingles rippled up and down, making James shiver heatedly.

Chad engulfed James's cock in his mouth once more and James felt inebriated. He groaned, clamping his mouth shut before a scream could escape him. James felt like he was melting, so good did Chad's mouth feel around his shaft. He thrust his pelvis up to encourage Chad to go faster, and Chad obliged.

James grabbed a pillow and pressed it down on his face. He screamed into it as his cock stiffened and his elation spilled over. He could feel himself fill Chad's mouth and he heard Chad swallow with a satisfied groan.

James pulled the pillow away, panting, staring down at Chad with as much desire to pleasure him as he had to be pleasured by him. He pulled Chad up, meeting his mouth for several moments of heavy kissing, tasting the remnants of his own semen on the insides of his husband's cheeks, before he lifted himself from the couch.

He led Chad to the position he wanted him in. Chad placed his hands on the back of the couch as James aligned himself with his anus.

'I know you like it when I take you from behind, baby. I know your ass loves fucking my cock.'

Chad moaned anticipatedly as James teased his entrance, craning his neck to stare at him with greed in his eyes. James slowly slid inside Chad, his dick still wet with saliva and ready, and Chad exhaled loudly. James grabbed Chad's erection with his free hand, as the other held onto Chad's chest, and he began to pound his ass.

'Oh, yes, fuck me,' Chad moaned. 'Fuck me good, baby, yes!'

James pumped him hard, thrusting back and forth. Chad's cock stiffened in his hand. James moved his left hand to grab Chad's, interlacing their fingers from over them, and he admired their rings as he pounded him. Chad pulled the pillow to him and placed it in front of him, though he looked back at James.

James bent forward, his mouth meeting Chad's, and Chad creased his eyebrows – James knew he was close. Chad turned, burying his face in the pillow, and a muffled scream escaped his lips. James did not ejaculate this time, but the pleasure he felt from hearing and feeling Chad come made him orgasm all over again, a wave rippling through his body just as intense as the first orgasm.

James kissed the back of Chad's neck, breathing gruffly, as Chad erupted onto his hand and all over the couch.

Their lips met again and Chad turned himself around – James's cock gently slipped out of Chad's ass with a sloosh. James lowered himself and took Chad's cock in his mouth like it was a popsicle and sucked it clean. Then he wrapped his arms around Chad, kissing him feverishly, and the two men wept again, their tears mingling.

James tasted the salty warm tears as he ate Chad's face. It made him chuckle while also clenching his heart.

'I promise,' Chad whispered. And he needn't repeat the details – James knew.

'I promise too,' James whispered back.

They moved to the bed, after cleaning the couch and themselves, and wrapped their arms around each other.

'You feel so good, baby,' Chad breathed.

'Right back atcha,' James sighed, still feeling elated.

His heart was still yearning, he was still hurting, but like any other fight they'd had, that would soon pass, and only their love would remain.

* * *

James awoke in Chad's arms, their naked bodies flush against each other, and he breathed in deeply, comforted by how they held their embrace. Then the events of the past days flooded back into his mind with a pang and his hold around Chad tightened.

'I'm not going anywhere,' Chad whispered into his neck. He kissed his skin gently before pulling away to lean their foreheads together.

James opened his eyes to see Chad peering at him. 'Neither am I,' James confirmed. He kissed Chad, opening his mouth to take his lips as his breakfast, and the two husbands made out for a while.

James let out a dissatisfied groan, feeling his body ready for Chad – and feeling Chad ready for him – all over again.

'As much as I'd love to make love to you again,' admitted James, 'it would be rude for one of us not to make an appearance upstairs, and that's going to have to be me. It's far too open with far too many windows to be safe for you right now.'

'Just be sure to bring me some breakfast,' Chad said, taking a nibble of James's lip and pulling gently on it.

James chuckled. 'You sure you aren't already having it?'

Chad hum-chuckled. 'I am certain that if I were having you for breakfast, you'd already be roaring.'

James felt a pulse in his groin at the thought and he bit his lower lip – Chad was just so sexy. Despite his continuous desire, James reluctantly pulled away and dressed. Then, he proceeded to make his way upstairs where Olivia and her fiancé, Benton, were having an elaborate brunch.

'Glad you could join us,' said Olivia, inviting James to sit with them. 'I hope everything worked out between you and Chad.'

James felt his cheeks get warm. 'Yeah,' he replied.

'Good,' declared Benton, though his reply sounded more like a 'Good riddance!' than anything else.

'The two of you can stay here as long as you need, if . . . that's what you need,' Olivia offered.

'You're letting your ex stay here?' complained Benton. 'Olivia, that guy's James Sharpe. He's trouble.'

'I trust him, it'll be fine. It's just for a few days.'

James glanced at Benton who was glowering at him. He'd wait to catch Olivia alone to give her the chèque for the damages on the wall downstairs.

'It's okay. This isn't something I can run away from. I need to face this head-on. But thanks. It means a lot that I had a place to stay last night. It was the safest place for us.'

'Of course.'

'We'll leave at sundown,' added James.

'Why at sundown? Why not this morning?' demanded Benton.

Olivia and James hesitated. 'You know how it is with these mobster types.' Olivia caressed Benton's hand. 'Don't ask questions.' Olivia turned to James. 'I don't need to know. You just do what you gotta do and stay safe.'

'Thanks. I appreciate that.' James looked at Benton. 'I'm really happy for you, you know. Olivia deserves a good man like you who's not part of . . . what *I'm* a part of. You take good care of her.'

Benton snorted. 'Yeah. Thanks.'

They finished eating, making idle chit-chat, and then James brought some food down to Chad, who was dressed and sitting on the couch, looking down at his phone, smiling.

Chad lifted his phone. 'Paige.' He read aloud, "Hey babes, hope all is well. Tell me how everything went."

'I'm sure she doesn't literally mean everything,' teased James. Chad chuckled, taking a bite of the bacon James had brought. 'Are you going to be okay without . . . you know, blood?'

Chad met James's eyes and the werewolf's stomach fluttered seeing the lust in Chad's eyes. 'You're my husband, you've let me suck you before, have you not?'

James grinned. 'If what you need is a werewolf's blood to tide you over, you can suck me.' James leaned towards Chad, bringing his lips close, and purred, 'And then you can suck me.' Chad playfully hit him with a pillow. 'He-ey,' laughed James, 'you're the one talking in innuendos.'

Chad popped a piece of melon in his mouth in a very suggestive manner. The way he chewed it made the heat rise in James's body. Chad took another piece of melon, holding it at his lips as he spoke. 'Accuse me of starting it, and I'll show you how I star—'

James's phone vibrated. He sighed, refocusing, but still feeling very hot. He looked down at the screen and sobered. 'Right, Ian.' He felt guilty for just disappearing on everyone and not giving any news to them. James read the text: *Call me or I'm going to kill you myself.*

Chad let out a laugh. 'You should've heard him last night.' He popped the melon in his mouth.

'You should've heard him and Rayan the other day. Those two have it hard for each other.'

'Oh, did they declare their love for each other, then?'

'Okay, so, there they were . . .' James repositioned himself to sit facing Chad, one knee up on the couch, talking to Chad like he was some gossiper. He recounted the whole story of how it all went down.

'No way!' Chad popped a grape in his mouth. 'That's hot. Wish I'd seen it.'

'Shut up,' James chided teasingly. 'I should give him a call.'

'Let's do a double date,' suggested Chad. 'Well, triple, since your bodyguards have to be there too. You, me, Paige, Evan, Ian and Rayan.'

'Tonight?' asked James. Chad nodded. 'That would be nice.'

Chad texted Paige as James called Ian. The werevamp gave him an earful, and then happily agreed to the triple date. James could hear the relief, anger, suppressed tears, and the joy in Ian's voice as he went through the emotions.

James chuckled, looking at Chad. 'Ian says he tried to dash after you but you're one hell of a fast vampire.'

Chad responded playfully, 'There's a time for speed, and there's a time to' – he elongated his next words – *'take things slow.'*

'I heard that,' Ian complained. He reiterated, 'As a werewolf, my speed was unrivalled. As a werevamp, you'd *think* I'd be able to keep up with a vampire!'

'You just need to keep up with me,' James heard Rayan tease.

Ian chuckled before reconfirming for the date and hanging up.

Chad sent Paige a picture of Ian that James had forwarded to him. Ian and Rayan had seen Paige the other night, so James was confident they would recognise her easily if they arrived before he and Chad did. James and Chad also each forwarded the address of the restaurant James wanted to treat them to – it was an elegant place with fine cuisine.

Chad smiled at James, chewing his breakfast food and looking excited. It filled James with such happiness, he was bursting, and part of the hurt that still lingered subsided instantly.

* * *

James and Chad left right as the sun was setting and drove back to town. They arrived near 10:00 PM. James parked in front of the restaurant across the street. He looked over at Chad and placed his hand on his thigh, smiling and squeezing. Chad bit his lower lip – his husband's touch felt electric.

'Careful, you'll get me going again and we're here for a date with our friends.' Chad had gone too long without James's touch and already needed him again, but . . . 'We can't have them wait too long.'

James chuckled, 'Oh, all right.' He leaned towards Chad and pecked him on the cheek.

'I'm looking forward to tonight,' Chad expressed, referring to their triple date. 'I want you to properly meet Paige. She's really sweet.' Chad furrowed his brows in thought. 'So are the chocolate bars I buy at the shop. I . . . must admit I've become quite addicted to them. I even asked her to bring me one for dessert tonight.'

'Hey, you just wait until you try their *crème brulée*,' said James as he reached to grab a suit jacket that rested on the backseat. 'I know you liked their *tiramisù* last time, but I'm telling you, their *crème brulée* is to die for, it just melts in your mouth.'

'If you're done making me salivate, then,' Chad motioned his hands out as if to shoo him away. Chuckling, the two husbands got out of the car.

As soon as Chad closed the door, something slammed into him from behind and the air left his lungs as he was pushed up against the car. On the other side, James was also rammed into the side of the car. Chad pushed back against his attacker as James extended his claws. Chad brought his arm up to block a fist that came at his face, while James attempted to turn around.

Something hard hit Chad's head and little black dots danced in his vision. He heard the screech of scratched metal and a muffled grunt. He used his vampire abilities to refocus but then a wet cloth was pressed against his face. Chad immediately began to feel lightheaded, the substance so strong, undoubtedly enhanced by poisons, even his vampiric abilities could not counter it. Chad's limbs grew numb before going limp, and everything went dark.

* * *

Head throbbing from whatever had hit him, Chad opened his eyes slowly. He was in a dim-lit room, slumped on a metal chair, his hands bound behind him in thick metal cuffs. His feet were also bound, but to large metal chains that tied them together.

In front of him, several feet away and facing him, sat James, bound in the same manner. The werewolf's head lolled to the side as he moaned in discomfort.

Chad's heart dropped to his stomach – there was only one person who would do this.

James opened his eyes and they widened. He met Chad's gaze and his eyebrows drew together in sorrow.

'Good morning!' Troy's heavy boots resounded in the echoing chamber. 'Well, not quite morning yet, but it soon will be. And a new dawn will I bring to the werewolf kind.'

James looked up at Troy in defiance as the other Alpha loomed above him. James spat at his feet.

'New dawn, my ass.'

Troy backhanded James in the face. 'Quiet!' Chad's heart stopped for a beat. Troy grabbed James by the cheeks, squeezing. 'You're going to meet your end, and your weakness will be known to all our kind. The Alpha who barely lasted a season.' James merely glared back at him. 'You're a disgrace to all werewolves, James Sharpe.'

Troy let go of James's face and turned towards Chad. 'And you, Chad Sharpe, you call yourself a vampire. You're just a werewolf fucker.'

Chad chuckled mirthlessly. 'That I am. A Sharpe fucker. So what of it?'

Troy punched Chad in the gut so hard, Chad felt like he was going to puke.

'Chad!' cried James.

Troy laughed sinisterly.

Chad's mind whirled as he tried to regain his bearings. If Troy was working with Constantia, then perhaps she had taught him much more than Troy was letting on.

'What the hell do you want, Troy?' demanded James.

Troy turned back to James. 'Your pack under my control, your alliance destroyed, your pitiful pleas to end your life.'

Troy's fist cracked against James's face and he followed through with a punch to his gut. The enemy werewolf was exuding his strength.

James fought against his bonds, extending his claws and pulling outwards.

'These are werewolf-and-vampire-proof,' stated Troy. 'You won't break free from these.'

James roared at Troy, snarling and baring his pointed teeth. Troy growled in response, sending a warning shot from his gun at the floor by James's feet. He punched James in the face again.

'Stop it!' cried Chad.

James spat blood on the floor. The swollen cut on his lip was healing but Troy knew how to hit hard enough to cause prolonged pain.

'I'm going to correct the error I made when I failed to kill you,' Troy sneered in James's face. 'How does it feel knowing you're about to meet your end, James Sharpe?'

'No!' Chad panicked. Troy punched James again. 'Stop it!'

Troy hefted his elaborate weapon and brought it to level. Chad's fear chilled his blood and his stomach twisted in knots.

Before he knew what he was doing, Chad was shouting at Troy, hoping against all odds he had deduced correctly.

'*Dēsiste!*' Chad shrieked, his voice pitched high in panic. '*Dēsiste statim!*' His heart hammered in his chest.

Troy paused and slowly turned his head towards Chad. Chad met his gaze, the passion he felt for James and the desire to save his life flaring in his eyes. Chad hung his mouth open so Troy could see him in full vampiric mien, eyes paled and canines extended.

'*Tū quis es quī iubēas me, vampīre?*' Troy replied. His Latin was somewhat accented, but Chad had guessed correctly. This put them on the same level, a different level to James, and Chad could negotiate with Troy without James's objections.

James stared at them, trembling in fear. Chad, for his part, found that a resolute calm had taken over him, and his body no longer shook.

'*Scio te Constantiam consociāre.*' Chad stated, his eyes never leaving Troy's.

'What?' breathed James. 'What's going on? What about Constantia?'

'*Scio eam finem,*' Chad went on, his jaw tight as Troy listened to him, gaze intent, '*quoniam quondam amans fui. Cūr ālium lupum caedas? Quōmodo bellum inter nostrum genera hoc incendet?*'

Troy chuckled, a dangerous smile creeping on the side of his mouth as he turned to face Chad fully. His response was mocking, and dripping with condescension. '*Igitur quid agam, eh?*'

Chad's eyes landed on James, who looked as confused as he did scared. This time, when Chad spoke, he kept his eyes on James. In his heart, he was telling him *I'm sorry.* Out loud, he voiced, '*Vicem me caede.*'

Eyes still flared and staring at his husband, Chad let out a shaking breath. There, he had said it, he had given himself up to save the man he loved.

'Chad?' James asked hesitantly, his face falling – he could no doubt sense Chad's intent, that was how intense their bond was.

Troy opened his mouth, amused by Chad's demand. He took a few steps towards him.

'*Mīrus est. Meam attentionem tū habes, perge.*'

Chad met Troy's gaze once more. Now he was shaking again, but he took a calming breath and laid out his arguments. '*Favorem cum muliēre quī dūcit tuum factionem pōtieris, etiam sempiternō perpetuābis bellum. Etiam, vulnerābis James, et in statu cresces.*'

Troy whooped a laugh. 'Haha! Impressive.'

James shook his head. 'Chad, what's going on? What was that exchange about?'

Troy hefted his weapon onto his back and clapped his hands together, slowly circling the two husbands. His grin was frightening, and excitement lit his eyes.

'Your husband's a noble one, James,' Troy expressed joyously as he kept his eyes on Chad. 'Consider yourself fortunate that I like his arguments.'

'What? What did you say? Chad, baby, what have you done?' mewled James.

'He's given himself up for you, James.'

Troy quickly drew his revolver and pressed the muzzle against Chad's temple – the weapon wasn't silver, but shot at point-blank like this, Chad had no chance of surviving. Chad shut his eyes tightly, bracing himself for what was to come.

* * *

It felt like James's heart had stopped.

'I could kill you right here and now,' Troy spoke deliberately, 'but where would the fun be in that, eh? No, I want to see you suffer and make a ritual out of this.' Keeping his gun pressed against Chad's head, he bent low from behind him and smirked at James.

Chad opened his eyes, tears sparkling through them. 'I'm sorry, James,' he whispered.

'Chad, baby, why?' cried James.

'Because I'm selfish,' wept Chad, 'and I would rather die than go on living eternally without you, James.'

'Baby!' James sobbed. The declaration at once chilled and heartened James, causing his entire body to quake in fear. James felt if Chad died, his life would end too. 'So you're sacrificing yourself for me?'

'I'm sorry, baby.' Chad's breath trembled. 'I love you too much. I'm done losing the ones I love.'

'But, baby, I'd rather die than live without you,' James pleaded.

'I can't bear to live in a world without you, James. Never once in all my existence did I want to marry before I met you. You changed that – you changed *me!* Of all those I have loved – and I've loved deeply – I have never loved anyone more than I love you.'

James felt hot tears brim his eyes, the sting blurring his vision. He felt like he could no longer breathe, and his lungs burned and squeezed as he stopped drawing in breath. Chad squeezed his eyes shut and tears poured down his face. James heaved in a sharp breath.

Troy laughed in his throat. 'Oh, how I love seeing you suffer, James Sharpe.' He grinned wickedly. 'I want to prolong your suffering. And yours!' he added, shoving his gun against Chad and stepping away. 'I will show no mercy, for I have nothing but contempt for you, vampire.'

Troy casually spoke words James could only assume were in Latin. '*Morte quam inferimus inimicis. Pūritās restituētur. Tenebrārum inferos dominabimur.*'

Other voices echoed the last phrase, as though it were a prayer.

Something was pulled over James's head and he could no longer see. He began shouting and kicking frantically before a cloth wreaking of the familiar smell of chloroform mixed with an enhancing agent was pressed against his nose and mouth, making him dizzy, and everything went dark.

* * *

James awoke to slaps on his face as he was being dragged, head no longer hooded. The blaring morning sunlight blinded him, small waves mere feet away lapping and receding, and he drew in a sharp breath, gasping aloud as he realised where they were.

His hands were shackled behind his back, his legs equally bound. He was bent forward, feet dragging on the ground as enemy werewolves carried him from under his arms.

James was pushed down onto one of the larger rocks, his pants ripped and knees scraped. The near instant healing did nothing to quell the pain in his heart.

James struggled against his bonds, watching as they brought Chad to his knees in front of him and the hood was removed from his head.

Chad winced against the sunlight, looking down. James's mouth felt dry, he wanted to scream, and yet he could only stare. He tried to control his breath and opened his mouth to speak, but nothing came out.

'You're going to watch as your lover dies – as werewolves kill him,' sneered Troy. 'And then, vampires are going to kill *you*.' James's heart sank even lower. 'Your bodies will be found and the war will be reignited.'

'You agreed I would die *instead* of him!' Chad hissed. He began sweating and panting, a sickly pallor taking over his features. James's heart pounded against his chest to the beat of his fear.

Troy spread out his arms, circling the two captives. 'This is the moment we've been waiting for, a ritualistic death. The war will commence anew, and vampires and werewolves will be pure again. The fae will return into hiding and exile, and we will vie for who is the dominant kind. Bloodshed will determine the outcome.'

'*Mendācium!*' Chad shouted, his voice strained. 'You lied!' He glared up at Troy. 'You have no honour.'

'Then let's test yours.' Troy smirked. He walked over to Chad, who was now rocking forward, moaning softly, his jaw tight.

As his werewolves watched on, surrounding them and standing guard, Troy unshackled Chad's legs and then his hands.

Chad fell forward, bracing himself on a rock with his hands, his fingers tense. He drew in several laboured breaths but did not move.

'Chad, baby!' wept James. 'Attack them – what are you waiting for? Drink their blood – there may still be a chance that you survive this.'

'I . . . have a responsibility to the pack as the Partner-Alpha now.' Chad's eyes remained on the rocks. 'I refuse to kill them. If I drink blood to survive this – because what I need is human blood – to have enough werewolf blood . . . that werewolf will die.' James exhaled slowly. 'And if I do that,' Chad went on, lifting his face to meet James's gaze, 'I break the oath I made to the pack – to *our* pack.'

'But he lied to you,' sobbed James. 'You did all this to save my life, and now once you're dead, he's going to kill me. If we die, the war is reignited either way, by them or by us. This is your chance – *our* chance – to survive.'

'I made a promise to the pack,' repeated Chad. 'I went down on my knee and swore an oath.' Chad's breathing became heavy and ragged.

'Chad,' James mewled.

James faintly became aware of the werewolves chanting a Gregorian theme in Latin.

'They're testing me, James.' The flare in Chad's eyes dimmed. He was trembling. 'Either we live but we start the war, or we die as heroes, and the war may never start.'

James let out a sob.

Chad continued with more effort. 'They want us to start this war. I won't give that to them. They've already taken too much.'

'And even if it's self-defence, it would mean dishonouring the oath we made,' concluded James, despair overpowering him.

'I could not live with myself if I broke that oath. I'm sorry. That oath means enough to me to sacrifice my life,' admitted Chad.

James's heart broke. 'And if you die, then I don't want to continue to live without you.'

James cursed his fate. He cursed his husband for being right, cursed him for his stubbornness, cursed him for his loyalty, cursed him for his sacrifice. James let out a series of elongated sobs. He wanted to be the one to die first and have his suffering end.

Chad's brows creased together in silent lament. He winced in pain as his skin began to break out in welts. His breathing became shallow. James wanted to reach for him, and his shackles felt heavier than ever as he struggled against them behind his back. Chad lifted his hand towards James before it fell again, and he breathed out a loud pained gasp.

'I love you, James Sharpe,' he whispered.

'I love you, Chad Sharpe,' James whispered through tears.

Chad coughed. 'James,' he managed, fear in his eyes. His breathing was rougher and his entire body was trembling.

'Baby,' James wept. Chad wretched and gagged. 'Oh my god,' James closed his eyes for a moment. Chad's skin now quickly welted, burning under the sweltering sunlight.

Chad's voice was faint when he repeated, 'James, baby . . . I love you.'

James heaved. 'Chad, I love you.'

Chad collapsed to the ground, convulsing in agony. James's stomach lurched at the sight, and all he could do was watch while tears poured down his face.

CHAPTER THIRTEEN

Something shiny whipped past James's nose and hit one of the guarding werewolves in the face. This one slapped his hand to his cheek, startled, and whelped. Whatever hit him, left a circular black mark. Another one of those things zipped by – James reflexively winced, his survival instincts kicking in despite his despair – it landed on the exposed chest of another werewolf, who shouted out in panic.

'What the fuck is wrong with you?' Troy complained.

Another whizz. And another. And soon, several of the werewolves were clutching themselves, frantic, or already down on the ground, writhing in agony.

James's heart raced – he didn't know what was going on, but he recognised the effects of silver, even while being too weak to perceive the glittering poison – every werewolf that got hit had inky marks spreading on their skin – and all James could do was look towards Chad, whose mouth was foaming in reaction to the sun exposure.

Something dashed before James – no, someone – and slammed into Troy, sending him to the ground. Then a reflective sheet was thrown over Chad and another being materialised, shimmering before James and kicking one of the werewolves in the groin and sending him whimpering back. The werewolf tripped and fell backwards onto the rocks.

James glanced up. Ian punched through another werewolf, his fist emerging bloody from behind his opponent's back. The werewolf's eyes grew vacant before he fell dead on top of the rocks.

Rayan coruscated between female and male forms, kicking and punching werewolves left and right, dispatching those closest to Chad and James.

Troy staggeringly pushed himself up to his feet, backing away and staring at Ian in disbelief.

'How?' he breathed, the fear apparent in his eyes.

Ian bared his teeth, canines extending, and hissed in Troy's face.

'Fuck!' Troy cursed in alarm.

Ian dashed him, but the Alpha dodged and bounded away, abandoning the scene.

'You fucking coward!' Ian shouted angrily.

The werevamp dashed behind James – James heard a sickening squelch before another werewolf hit the rocks with a thud. Ian crouched behind James, lockpicking his shackles and before James knew it, he was free.

Reflectively, James reached for Chad, placing his arms under him, and scooped him up.

'Duck!' Rayan grabbed James by the shoulder and pushed him down. James protectively brought Chad's body to his bosom.

Another silver pellet swooshed over James's head. Ian sidestepped and jumped up, and the projectile landed on the head of a downed but still alive werewolf who had started to get back up. This one fell flat onto his stomach again.

Rayan took a stance before James and Chad and grabbed a werewolf's head, the fae twisted with a snap – the man fell dead at Rayan's feet.

Ian punched out both arms to either side, impaling two werewolves. They slumped on Ian's arms. Ian pulled his arms free and the dead werewolves fell to the rocks.

James gaped at Rayan and Ian before turning and running to the trees where he knew the shade would be better for Chad than out on the rocks.

'Over here!' a small voice whispered loudly.

James looked up to see Paige and a young man standing beneath some dense trees. Paige held out her hand to her partner, open palm up, and the young man placed a silver coin on it. Paige took aim, bringing her arm back, and flicked the coin with her fingers as her arm followed-through with the movement.

James gently lay Chad down on the underbrush nearby but at a safe distance from the whizzing silver coins. A roar told him Ian and Rayan were still fighting the other werewolves. James pulled the heavy blanket with the reflecting cover from Chad's face. The vampire's eyes were closed and his head was jerking this way and that.

'Chad. Chad, baby, can you hear me?' James took Chad's face in his hands – he was looking more and more ashen by the minute.

Paige and her friend joined James by Chad's side.

'He needs blood.' James bowed his head. 'And for him to survive this, he needs human blood.'

'Yours won't be enough?' the young man asked – James assumed this was Evan.

James shook his head. 'Not for this, no.'

'He needs human blood, right?' confirmed Paige. She placed her wrist in front of Chad's mouth.

James grabbed her wrist abruptly and pulled it away as Chad bared his fangs, emitting a primal sound from his throat, eyes always shut tight.

'His raw instincts are kicking in, he could hurt you,' James warned her.

'I'm not scared.' Paige pulled out a chocolate bar from her purse and held it close to Chad's nose. 'Chad, it's me, Paige. Do what you need to, just keep me alive, okay?' She took a quick beat. 'I trust you.'

Again, she placed her wrist near Chad's face and Chad opened his mouth, canines ready. He lifted his head and sank his fangs into Paige. She yelped, wincing.

Chad drank for a while. Ian and Rayan returned, the fae transfiguring into female form.

'The rest of them escaped,' growled Ian, glaring in the direction their enemies had run as he used a cloth to wipe the blood off his arms and hands.

'We staked those we killed,' said Rayan, discarding a branch.

Ian turned to James and his eyes landed on Paige. 'God, Paige!' he exclaimed.

'It's fine,' Paige strained. She was beginning to look pale, but she bravely held her hand and let Chad drink her blood.

Chad pulled away and lay his head back down, eyes closed the whole time.

'How are you feeling, Paige?' Evan asked, placing his hand on her back, concern in his eyes.

'Well, I'm not dead and I haven't turned, so I guess I'm okay.'

James gaped at her, admiring her bravery.

'Hm, I'll have that chocolate bar now,' Chad mumbled.

'Chad!' They all exclaimed.

'Baby!' James breathed.

Chad reached towards him and took his hand. Then Chad opened his eyes and a small grin crept onto his face. James stared at him for a moment before he plunged to his lips, Chad pulling him closer to him as they kissed hungrily, desperate for each other.

They pulled away, breathless. Chad winced. He looked at Paige. 'Thank you. My body is healing me already.' He stretched a hand towards her. She smiled, reaching her hand the rest of the way, but instead of holding her, Chad reached for the chocolate bar and grabbed it. He unwrapped it and began to eat.

'I was serious, you know,' he said with his mouth full. 'I've grown addicted to these.'

James let out a tearful laugh. He looked from Ian to Rayan, and to Paige and Evan. 'How did you know? How did you find us?'

'It was all Paige,' said Ian.

* * *

'James still won't answer his phone. Damnit! This isn't like them to be late like this,' complained Ian, worry nagging at him.

Paige shifted uneasily in her chair, looking down at her phone. 'Chad's not answering either. Something's wrong.'

'Agreed.'

'Right, we have to do something.'

Without preamble, the four of them stood from the table and exited the restaurant. Outside, Ian saw James's car, parked and untouched. They approached it.

Rayan reached for the door and opened it. She gasped. 'Unlocked.'

'That's not normal,' declared Ian.

'What does that mean?' asked Paige. 'Something happened right when they got out of the car, or what?'

Evan bent down and picked a suit jacket up off the asphalt – James's suit jacket.

'These paint scratches look like claw marks,' noted Rayan as Ian drew his conclusion.

Ian clenched his jaw and his stomach twisted into a knot. 'They were taken.'

Paige and her boyfriend had a whispered exchange. 'We need to stop by the apartment,' declared Paige.

The apartment wasn't far.

'Where the hell *are* they?!' Ian growled as Paige and Evan walked into her room. 'How the hell are we supposed to find them!'

'I think it's safe to assume Troy has them, and I think they're going to take them to the river,' deduced Paige, as she pushed aside a pile of clothes from the foot of her bed.

'The river? How do you reckon that?' asked Rayan, who was removing her clip-on earrings.

'Chad told me that when he goes,' Paige called out from her room, 'sometimes he can hear them chanting, sometimes even see where they are.'

Evan lifted the mattress and, crouching, Paige reached under it.

'He says it's a good distance from his location,' Paige went on. 'He used his vampiric sight to see them, but if we go to the place where he took me once, it's a good starting point.'

'We know the place,' said Ian, tensing up. He absentmindedly put his hand to his left upper chest. 'It's where . . .' He had rather not think about that night.

Paige produced a cylinder of plastic-wrapped coins. 'I knew this investment was going to pay off someday,' declared Paige. 'Didn't think it would be this, but I'm okay with that.'

Paige rose and walked back towards Ian, showing him the cylinder she held – silver.

'Investment?' Ian stared at the silver coins, wondering what her game plan with them was.

'Way cheaper than Gold,' said Paige. Ian's eyes widened. 'Don't worry, I'll explain on the way.'

Rayan looked at Evan. 'You have pants I can borrow? And a pair of sneakers?'

'Uh, yeah.'

Evan quickly tossed a pair of pants and some sneakers at Rayan, who slipped the pants on from under her skirt. 'But why the river?' she asked Paige as Evan entered his room.

Paige chewed her lip nervously. 'If these guys are ritualistic, and they really want to hurt James, then they'll hurt Chad, and if they want to hurt Chad, they'll expose him to the sun.'

'How are you deducing all this? Are you some sort of vampire-werewolf expert all of a sudden?' Evan asked as he reappeared from his room with a heavy blanket that had a reflector sheet on one side.

'I talked a lot with Chad and I was there when we ran into Troy, remember? What he said, what Chad said, I just . . . I just know it, that's all.'

'If you're wrong, though . . .' Ian warned. Then, 'But it makes sense. It's better than coming up empty as we have.' He nodded – they had an action plan. 'Okay, but we should be careful on our approach. We don't want to give ourselves away.'

Rayan put the sneakers on and with a flicker of magic morphed into male form. 'It fits, it'll work.' Rayan switched back to female form.

'Bruh, now that's cool,' admitted Evan.

'What's *that* for?' asked Ian, pointing at Evan's heavy blanket.

'Uh, short explanation or scientific explanation?' asked Evan.

'Short.'

'It's going to block out the sun and protect Chad.'

'I'm all set,' Rayan announced, looking ready for combat. Paige and Evan nodded to Ian, confirming they too were ready to find the Sharpe husbands.

'Right,' said Ian, 'let's move!'

* * *

Chad's lips curved into a mild smile. His face was regaining its natural sheen and his skin was beginning to heal. 'You're brilliant, Paige, you know that?'

Paige blushed and shrugged, smiling. 'I have my moments.'

'Chad, baby, can you stand? Can you walk?'

'I'm feeling rather weak, at the moment,' replied Chad. 'I think I need a werewolf's strong arms to carry me.'

'I'll carry you anywhere, baby.'

James placed his arms under Chad and lifted him off the ground. Chad wrapped his arms around James's neck, still chewing on his chocolate bar. James kissed him, tasting the sweetness of the chocolate as his tongue twined with Chad's. He pressed for more before Chad could pull away, savouring his husband's – and the chocolate's – taste.

'See what I mean?' Chad said when he pulled away.

'Give me a bite of that,' James demanded playfully before taking a small bite. He covered Chad's head with the blanket as he carried him out of the woods.

* * *

Chad awoke to feel the soft sheets of his bed beneath him and the familiar scent of James's musk wrapped around him. He breathed in, feeling much more alive than before. He hadn't realised he'd dozed off in James's arms.

Chad opened his eyes to see James lying next to him, a protective arm holding him close – James's eyes were closed, though his features seemed strained with worry. His beaten face had healed now, only a few remnants of bruises remained where he got hit harder and would probably resolve within the hour. Chad, on the other hand, would require another day or two, as sun exposure was not fast-healing, especially considering how long Chad spent out in it – he felt like he was recovering from a bad flu.

On the edge and side of the bed sat Paige and Evan, absorbed by something on the phone they were scrolling through. Julian and Liam sat on the small couch, leaning the sides of their heads together and staring at the floor, while Ian and Rayan stood whispering to each other, grave expressions on their faces.

Chad tried to sit up and winced. James immediately stirred, his eyes frantic and wide.

'Chad, baby!'

Everyone's attention turned to Chad. James helped him straighten and sat up beside him, holding his hand in both of his.

Liam bounced up and rushed to the hall, calling out, 'He's awake!' The others moved towards the bed.

'Oh, thank god!' Rachel cried as she and Keisuke entered the room. Hikaru was bumbling in Rachel's arms and reaching a small hand towards Chad.

Chad reassured them. 'I'm okay, I'm alive. My stomach feels a bit woozy, but I'm otherwise all right.'

Rachel bent forward a bit to allow Hikaru to poke Chad's nose. Chad noticed the tears in the mother's eyes. He smiled fondly.

'God, Chad, we were so worried. I mean, who's going to tease me about threesomes and annoy the hell out of all our husbands if not you?'

Chad reached up and wiped a tear from Rachel's face with a knuckle. Rachel took his hand and squeezed as Keisuke merely smiled, his eyes also glinting. It truly warmed Chad's heart to know how much they cared.

'Someone here has to keep reminding Julian of how jealous he is of me,' Liam teased tearfully.

'When we got back, Rachel and Keisuke did what was needed so you could have a bit more human blood,' explained Julian as he approached him.

Chad's heart swelled with affection. 'I appreciate the two of you contributing to my healing by giving your blood – truly.'

'We only did what was necessary,' stated Keisuke, his diplomatic voice cracking with emotion. 'You're a cherished member of this household, Chad. We'll always provide what we can when we can.'

Rachel bent and kissed Chad's forehead. Keisuke took the vampire's hand and squeezed, muttering in Japanese, '*Continue to stay alive, my friend.*' Keisuke and Rachel stepped back. Liam quickly took her place to bend and wrap his arms around Chad for a quick hug before pulling back.

Chad beamed at his friends, he simply could not stop smiling – he was so happy in this moment.

Julian looked Chad over and then blinked. 'When I heard what happened—' He pressed his lips together nervously. Chad nodded his understanding. 'Fuck, Chad . . . sometimes I can't stand you, but my god have you become family to me.' Julian sat down on the bed and gave Chad a hug, weeping. 'You're my kin, man.'

'As you are mine, Julian,' Chad said as they held their embrace. Julian pulled away, looking embarrassed.

Chad sniffed the air, becoming aware of a flowery aroma tickling his nose. 'What's that smell? It comes and goes but I can't place it.'

'Oh, it's my hand cream,' said Paige. 'I put some on your skin where you had some welts. It's got soothing lavender, calendula . . . a bunch of other ingredients. It really makes my hands soft – I figured it might help.'

Chad chuckled. He smelled his arm. 'It's nice,' he admitted. 'It masks my body odour.' Paige grinned, nodding her amused agreement.

Ian looked over at Chad. He jerked his head towards Paige. 'Should've seen her with her aim.'

Chad's smile widened. 'I *have* seen her aim. What is it you kids call it – on fleek?'

Paige squealed in delight and Hikaru imitated the squeal. Everyone laughed, looking very relieved.

James's eyes glittered with tears. 'Oh, baby, I love you so much.' He kissed Chad's hand again and again, kissing the ring on his finger.

Chad placed his hand on James's face. 'I'm sorry I gave myself up. I . . .'

'Don't apologise,' said James. 'We got through it, and we would have died together otherwise. I was so scared, baby, but . . . knowing how much you honour your promise to the pack, it only makes me love you more.'

'I also honour the promises I made to you, and I broke them when I—'

'That's not true. You honoured them.' James clenched his jaw in resolve and Chad understood his meaning.

'You keep making me fall in love with you all over again, too, baby.'

Chad winced loudly as his stinging blisters flared up. James reached for a wet cloth on the night table and lightly dabbed Chad's blistered arms. Chad winced again but then felt the cool water followed by the gentle stroke of James's hand.

James cupped Chad's cheek with his hand and stared deep into his eyes as he continued. Distracted by the fierce intensity of his gaze, Chad only felt flutters instead of the pain. Chad placed his hand on top of his husband's and closed his eyes as he turned his head and kissed the palm of James's hand. Then Chad remembered they were not alone, and his cheeks felt warm. James smiled, biting his lower lip – it tugged at Chad's heart with tender longing.

'Should we leave and let the two of you . . . ?' teased Julian.

Chad chuckled self-consciously. 'I'd love nothing more, but I'm afraid my wounds still need healing before I can indulge in my husband again.'

'Aw, you two are so sweet. I'm so obsessed!' Paige proclaimed with a delightful squeal.

Ian and Rayan walked over to the bed. 'We've put out an alert for Troy,' Rayan informed them.

'What a fucking coward,' Ian growled under his breath.

'Right – I know what will draw him out.' James pulled out his phone. 'Troy wants to play dirty? It's time to give him a taste of his medicine.'

James began recording, looking straight into the phone's camera. 'Troy. I, James Sharpe, challenge you. Face me, and if you defeat me, I will give you what you ask.' James stopped the recording. He passed his phone to Ian. 'Get this out online, and make sure, wherever Troy emerges, he meets us at the stadium.'

'Got it.'

James and Ian exchanged a few more words, and then Ian and Rayan left to continue their search and take care of the Alpha's business.

Chad scowled in puzzlement as Paige and Evan continued to scroll through a very familiar-looking phone. 'Is that mine?' he inquired.

'Oh, sorry,' said Paige, turning to face Chad again. 'We were looking through your wedding photos.' She flicked her wrist down. 'They're gorgeous. You guys look so hot in your suits. And, oh my god, babes, those eyes of yours, with the snow around you.' Page fanned herself, giggling, prompting a chuckle from everyone.

'You have an encrypted video on there, eh,' said Evan, leaning forward to glance at Chad past Paige before returning his attention to the phone.

'Oh, yeah, I forgot about that,' Chad realised. 'I received it sometime last year and then completely forgot to decrypt it, what with being Julian's best man, and then planning my engagement with James, helping with Rachel's wedding, helping with Hikaru's birth, actually marrying James . . . It's been an eventful year.'

'Add plus sign,' said Paige, drawing a plus sign in the air.

'I can decrypt it for you,' offered Evan. 'It's a simple encryption.'

'Oh my god, Evan, you're such a nerd, it's so hot!' laughed Paige.

Evan lifted his head and leaned towards Paige. 'I'll decrypt *you* later, babe,' Evan purred softly. Paige giggled. Everyone else couldn't help but laugh.

Rachel and Keisuke joined the others on the other side of the bed – as did Liam who squeezed in between Julian and Paige – finding a spot to sit on, and letting Hikaru crawl around between everyone.

'And there.' Evan announced. He handed Chad his phone.

Chad froze when he saw the face of the video's sender.

'Is that her?' Paige asked gently.

Chad looked up at the others. 'It's from Mandy.'

Liam and Julian exchanged a glance. Chad merely stared down at his phone.

Paige placed a hand on Chad's. 'You wanted closure. Maybe this is the closure you need.'

'I don't know.'

Chad took a few calming breaths before hitting play.

In the video, Mandy stared at the screen, pressing her lips together. Behind her was the familiar interior of the safehouse where she had been killed.

'Chad . . . hi,' she began. 'By the time you'll be seeing this message, well, you'll know what I've done. Either I'll have succeeded and then will be ending my life, or . . . Yeah, because at the end of it all, I intend to die. I first want to see this through, see vampires suffer.' Her face twisted in anger. 'I hate them, Chad – I hate them all. I hate what I am! I never asked for this.'

Her eyes reflected tears, and Chad's eyes stung with tears of his own.

'I hate them,' Mandy repeated. 'Except you.'

Chad let out a soft sob, closing his eyes tightly for a moment as Mandy continued.

'You're the only one I hope survives this, Chad. I know it makes me selfish, but, you're the only one I felt loved me . . . accepted me. You were like a brother to me.'

Chad brought his eyes back to the video. 'Every day that I exist, I loathe myself, Chad. I can't do it anymore, I can't . . . do this! I can't continue like this.'

Mandy paused. 'I hope they don't send you because I won't fight you. Whoever they send . . . I'll do what I have to.'

Julian let out a slow breath, and Chad saw that Liam held his hand tightly.

'But I don't want to fight you, Chad. I don't want to kill you. And since I want to end my existence anyway, I'll let you do what you have to.'

'Oh, Mandy,' Chad whispered.

'I just . . .' Mandy looked up and sighed. 'I should have died that night. I was wrenched from those I loved. My husband, my children. But you . . . you held me, caressed me, rocked me, made me feel like it would all be okay.' Mandy looked back at the screen. 'Except it wasn't. Those feelings never vanished. They only festered.'

'Why didn't you ever express it, share it with me?' wept Chad. 'We could have worked through it together and maybe you would have gotten over it.'

'And I could never accept what I became because of it,' Mandy went on. 'When this is all over, I hope you'll have gotten away to a safe place. Once I see it through . . .' She drew her brows together in thought.

'I haven't told Whitlock this. He's my descendant, did you know that? Yeah. But I haven't told anyone what I intend – only you, Chad. I'm going to stake myself. Once I see the end of the vampire kind – or as much of it as I can – because I'll take this as far as I can, this is just the start – but once I'm done, I'm going to run my heart through with my silver dagger and end my existence once and for all, and I'll die . . . the way I should have in the first place – murdered by a vampire.'

Chad placed a hand to his mouth and he coughed out a sob.

'I guess what I'm trying to say is . . . thank you, Chad, for making my existence at least a little tolerable for a time. And . . .' Mandy paused for a long time. 'I'm sorry.' She hesitated before ending the video.

Chad brought his hand to his eyes, letting his phone drop on the bed, and wept loudly. James pulled him into his embrace. Chad's blisters and welts burned, but the chagrin he felt was greater than the discomfort on his skin – he needed that little bit of comfort, the loving embrace of his husband.

Chad felt hands touch him, and knew his friends were conveying their sympathy and compassion. Chad was grateful, but all he could do was weep in his husband's arms.

* * *

James marched into the packed stadium. His husband, bodyguards, and friends following close behind him – Rachel and Keisuke had stayed home with the baby. They settled in seats near the stadium floor while James strode to the centre where Troy already awaited him.

'Glad to see you took the bait, Troy,' James sneered in his face, puffing out his chest.

Troy crossed his arms, glowering at James with disdain.

James backed several feet away from Troy. He looked up and called out loudly, roaring to be heard.

'Sharpe Pack, this man, this werewolf, this . . . *coward*' – he spat the word – 'tried to kill me, tried to kill my husband, by shackling us, and bringing us out into the sun.'

Gasps and oohs echoed throughout the crowd.

'This sorry excuse for a werewolf wants to hinder the alliance between werewolves and vampires. He wants to reignite the war of centuries past. And my husband—' James's voice cracked. He looked Chad's way. 'Had he drunk a werewolf's blood to survive, would have killed that werewolf.'

James returned his attention to the crowd. 'But because he knelt before you all and made a vow – an oath he claims he would not be able to live with himself had he broken – he did not fight back. Instead, he chose to sacrifice himself, because in that moment his honour meant more to him than his own life.'

James put extra emphasis on his next words. 'Even though in self-defence his actions would have been defendable and judged as tolerable by many of us who signed into this alliance, Chad, my husband – our pack's *Partner-Alpha* – chose to honour his oath to the pack and the alliance.'

James paused, bowing his head – he chose not to hide his tears from his pack. 'I nearly . . . lost him, and I would have been killed after I had watched him die.'

James saw pack members who were farther back searching for their Alpha's partner.

'As luck would have it, you're stuck with us as your Alpha and Partner-Alpha – we were saved . . . by a werevamp, a *fae*, and two *humans*.' He let that sink in. Then, he pointed at Troy. 'And this coward ran away. He – *you* – are a disgrace, Troy.'

James squared his shoulders and turned to face his nemesis.

'So now I challenge you, out in the open for all to witness, because unlike you, Troy, *I* have honour. But we fight not to win control of my pack or for me to give into your asinine demands. No, I challenge you, Alpha to Alpha, to finish what you started, to do things the way we should have in the first place.'

James strode towards Troy and stopped to keep several paces between them. 'We fight as werewolves, unarmed, and if I overpower you, I decide what becomes of you.'

The crowd cheered their agreement.

'And what do I get if I overpower *you?*' demanded Troy.

'You get to leave with your life,' declared James.

His pack roared for their Alpha. James cracked his knuckles and rolled his neck.

Troy leapt at James and the Sharpe Alpha was ready for him. Extending his claws, James grabbed Troy's arms, digging his nails in, and turned, flinging him. Troy landed several feet away, bouncing on the ground.

Troy stood anew, growling in anger. James extended an arm as Troy bounded towards him. Troy slashed at James's face. James turned away in the opposite direction only to realise at the last second it left him exposed. Troy slashed his side. James turned sideways and Troy slashed again, scratching James's back.

James shouted out as the pain pierced him before subsiding. James ran towards Troy and shoved him, head butting against the other Alpha's chest. The two landed on the ground and rolled a few times before coming to a stop, James on top of Troy – James had Troy pinned and he held him there.

'It's over, Troy.'

Troy pushed hard against James and they rolled again. This time, it was Troy who had James pinned beneath him. Troy delivered an uppercut to James's face as the enemy Alpha lifted himself off the ground – James's head jerked back. Standing anew, Troy kicked James in the face.

'Argh!' James brought his hand to his nose as blood spilled from it, causing his nostrils to congest before his nose could heal.

Troy hurled James to his feet only to kick him in the chest. Winded, James staggered back.

'It's over when I say it's over!' Troy reached into his jacket.

Suddenly, everything felt like it was moving in slow motion.

Troy shouted out. *'Morte quam inferimus inimicis!'*

He pulled out a shotgun with a muzzle large enough to house those horrid exploding pellets.

'Pūritās restituētur!'

The crowd gasped as Troy took aim, and James's blood ran cold.

Troy said more quietly, *'Tenebrārum inferos dominabimur.'*

James dove to the ground as a gunshot thundered through the stadium, whizzing past right above him where he had stood. It lodged into the ground several metres away.

'James!' cried Chad.

James's vision refocused in real time as Troy reloaded.

A familiar blur dashed between them and slammed into Troy, pushing him to the ground, chopping down with a ridge-hand strike at the hand that held the gun, and it clattered to the ground. Looming over him and taking a menacing step forward, Chad landed a kick to Troy's face. His eyes were flared white and canines extended.

'You have no honour!' Chad bellowed, his voice gruff with anger. 'You're a coward. You're no true Alpha!' He kicked him again, this time in the stomach. Chad balled his hands into fists, murder in his eyes. '*You're* the disgrace.'

Chad backed away from Troy and pointed towards the exit. 'Leave!' He leaned forward. 'This is your final warning before I decide to kill you.'

Troy rolled towards his weapon and reached for it so fast, James barely registered the movement. Troy aimed at Chad – and fired.

'CHAD!' screamed James, his voice shrill.

A blur zoomed before them and pushed Chad away before he stopped as the bullet hit flesh.

Liam staggered a few steps, crying out in pain. He clutched his shoulder and then cried out again.

'Argh, fuck! Fuck, that shit's painful.'

Troy shot at Chad again, and Liam moved and took that bullet too. Paige shrieked as Troy shot yet a third bullet and Julian cried out Liam's name.

Troy changed his angle, this time aiming at James, and shot within the same beat. James's heart thudded against his chest as he jerked out of the way, but he was too slow and the bullet reached him. At the last millisecond, Liam appeared, having dashed the few metres to stand before him, and took the hit for James, wincing and grimacing from the impact.

'Thanks,' James breathed.

'No problem.'

Troy reloaded and that was their chance.

James lunged forward, as did Chad, and kicked his hands hard, sending the weapon out of Troy's grasp.

Crowd members were rising from their seats, and a group of werewolves fled towards the exit.

'Stop them!' yelled Ian as he and Rayan darted after them.

James paused, his eyes going from Liam to Chad. Dozens of tiny pieces of shrapnel rained out of Liam with a sound akin to raining pebbles.

Liam glared at Troy who gaped in shock at Liam. The *Sui Generis Lamia* bared his fangs at him with an angry snarl, green eyes flaring – he was impressive, and James had so much appreciation for him at this moment.

'You told me I should be on your side, fighting for the purity of my kind,' Liam seethed. 'I am on the side of those who honour the lives of all the beings of all the realms.' Liam spread out his arms and shouted out. 'I am the *Sui Generis Lamia!*' He pointed at Troy. 'I declare you, Troy, my enemy, and thus the enemy of my coven, and of all vampire covens and werewolf packs who are part of the alliance with me.' He sneered. 'Because yes, I sign as an official representative of the alliance.'

Troy growled at Liam and bounded away like the coward he was. Liam dashed after him, as did Julian.

James stared at Chad who in turn stared back at him, both panting heavily. And then the two lunged forward, now locked in a passionate embrace, tears streaming down both their faces and mixing with their saliva as their tongues danced together.

EPILOGUE

'Hey, babes!' came Paige's voice as she pranced into the hall accompanied by Evan.

Chad acknowledged her. She gave him a hug and two little friendly pecks on his cheeks. His heart felt heavy at the moment, but at the same time, he felt release.

Chad clutched the large urn in his hands and looked at everyone who stood waiting for his signal.

Liam and Julian held hands, sober expressions on their faces. Julian had nearly lost his life last year, not to mention many of the events begun by the Cromwells and Mandy had brought the pair together – had brought everyone together.

Chad looked over at James. His husband offered him a tender smile. It had been five months now since Chad and James married, and a year more since Chad had proposed, since . . .

'I'm ready,' Chad announced softly.

'Let's go,' said Paige.

They drove down to the river and walked to the spot where Chad always went, the spot Chad had made his own. James stood by Chad's side, Liam and Julian a few steps away on his flank, Page and Evan on a rock beside Chad, and Ian and Rayan stood just a few paces behind.

With James by his side, Chad stepped up to the edge of the water and looked down at the urn. 'It's hard to believe all those ashes fit in this thing. I'm sure a lot of it is the safehouse and maybe only parts of it are Mandy.'

'Does it matter?' asked Paige. 'This is symbolic.'

'You're right,' agreed Chad. 'This is me letting go. I may not have had the closure I was looking for, but at least there were *some* answers. I now know that Mandy did care about me – and that I meant enough to her that she wished I wouldn't be the one sent to kill her, enough to wish I'd survive.'

Chad glanced at the water that reflected the crescent moon's light. 'I still have a lot of questions, questions I'll never have answers to, but I've come to realise that I don't need those answers. I can grieve Mandy's death *and* hate her for what she did, I can love her like a sister and be angry that she hurt me through her actions.'

Chad looked back at the urn. 'She cared about me, and through knowing that, I can find the closure I've been seeking.'

Chad turned to his friends, waiting to see if they had something they wanted to say. Liam shook his head. The blond man looked at Julian. Julian opened his mouth before closing it again. He looked down at his hand that was interlaced with Liam's.

'What she started, it led me to Nightly Glow Club,' said Julian, 'so I have to thank her for bringing me to the love of my life.' He looked up at Liam. 'But we could have met a different way too. I trusted her for the years that I knew her.'

Julian sighed, vivid blue eyes gazing out at the flowing river as it lapped and murmured softly.

'No one deserves to suffer what she had to live through, but that does not justify her actions. I don't regret being chosen to confront her, but I wish some things could have turned out differently.'

'I don't regret killing her,' said Liam, his voice tender, 'but I'm sorry at the same time.' His eyes met Chad's. 'Not sorry towards *her*, but towards *you*. Because despite what she did, she was your friend, a sister. I'd do any-thing to keep mine safe – I love Rachel to bits.'

Liam took a step towards Chad, his green eyes reflecting the colours of the water a few feet away. 'Chad, I'm sorry I killed Mandy. Because I know that even if you knew it had to be done, it hurt you to lose her. I'm the one who caused that.'

Chad's heart filled with warmth for his friend. 'No, you're not, Liam. *She* caused it. But thank you. You and Julian did what I could not, and I'm grateful for it. You did not hurt me, Liam,' he reassured again, '*she* did. I am . . . appreciative it was not me who was sent to do it.'

'Still, I'm sorry I killed your vampire sister.' The younger vampire had those puppy-dog eyes. It was endearing.

Chad gave Liam a wan smile. 'Accepted.'

James said nothing, but his presence close to Chad was the comfort Chad needed.

Chad lifted the lid off the urn. 'I don't know what lies after death for a vampire, but I hope you've found the peace you sought. If reincarnation is real, then I hope your next life will be a better one, a happier one, one filled with love without the woes that being a vampire might bring you.'

Chad walked right up to the river's edge, where small waves lapped gently on the rocks. He half-whispered, 'Goodbye, Mandy. I'm sorry too.'

Chad thrust the urn forward, scattering the ashes contained within it into the river – they flew with the wind, a drifting sprinkle of the past. Then he closed the urn and backed away a few paces. Placing the urn at his feet, Chad looked out at the water.

James immediately took hold of Chad's free hand, Liam and Julian came to stand on the other side of Chad, and Paige and Evan stepped closer, as did Ian and Rayan. Paige placed her hand on Chad's back.

The group looked out at the water and drifting ashes in silence for as long as Chad needed to remain there.

A tear ran down Chad's cheek, but he was content now. He felt like he had finally let go – or started to – like he could finally be free of his grief. And the pang in his heart associated with Mandy he'd so often felt, was gone.

When he was ready, Chad stepped away and turned his back to the water.

Ian pointed a thumb over his shoulder. 'Rayan and I are going to keep searching for Troy, try to track his scent.'

'We're joining them tonight,' declared Julian, 'see what the four of us can come up with.'

'All right, thanks,' said James.

'I'll see what I hear from people,' said Paige. 'Sometimes we hear gossip that sounds juicy at the shop, even if it isn't about anyone we know. If we hear anything weird, we'll call.'

'I appreciate that, thanks,' said James.

'My sister's still with Keisuke and the baby at the Matsuokas,' said Liam, 'and the three of them won't be back until next week.' He fidgeted, preoccupied. 'Troy knows Keisuke, though, he's seen him in a fight. I hope he or his pack won't follow them out of town.'

'I'm sure they'll be fine,' Chad reassured him. 'They're tough. And they'll call if there's anything.'

'Troy hasn't gone that far,' James contended. 'I can smell his lingering scent in the air in some areas of the city. He's gone underground, but he's still here somewhere. I trust you and your skills, Ian. I trust you'll find him – you've always had a knack for sniffing someone out. And I trust that Rachel, Keisuke, and the baby will be safe.'

Everyone nodded, and then left their separate ways.

* * *

James sat deep in thought at the foot of the bed. Chad looked relieved and ready to put everything else behind him.

'Rachel and Keisuke are out with the baby at the Matsuokas,' Chad began as though enumerating a list, 'and the others are off hunting.' Chad turned to James, grinning, 'We have the entire house all to ourselves. We can scream as loud as we want, baby.'

Chad's expression sobered – he must've noticed James's non-reaction. Heart hammering in his chest, James took a deep breath. He was so nervous about asking this, but he was so certain he wanted it.

'What's wrong, baby?' Chad approached James and took his chin in his hands, bringing his face up to meet his gaze.

'Chad, there's something I need to talk to you about.' James swallowed hard.

Chad nodded, looking nervous, and sat down beside James on the edge of the bed, his knees turned towards him. 'I'm listening.'

James took Chad's hands in his, staring down at them. 'I've been thinking about this long and hard. I . . .' He shifted his gaze to Chad, feeling the fire in his eyes. 'I want you to make me a werevamp.'

Chad's eyes widened. 'A werevamp! Are you certain?'

'I've never been more certain of anything in my life, Chad.' James caught himself – that wasn't entirely true. 'No, wait, that's not true. I am as certain of this as I am of my love for you.'

Chad blinked, holding James's hands more tightly. 'It's a great responsibility. It requires adapting.'

'I know. Perhaps I'd be more reluctant had I not seen someone turned or knew someone who was one, but I'm confident I'll adapt well.' His eyes reflected his ardency. 'Chad,' James tenderly placed his hand on Chad's face, gently rubbing his thumb, 'you told me you were done losing the ones you love.' Chad nodded once. 'You would never lose me. I am ready to spend eternity with you, to make this commitment to you. We would be together truly forever, not just a couple of centuries.'

James smiled, not just *knowing* how much he wanted this, but *feeling* it. 'I want this. I want to be a werevamp. To commit to you for . . . *forever* – and I want you to turn me.'

James suddenly realised that perhaps Chad was not ready for the commitment he was proposing. He bowed his head. 'I know it's one thing to commit yourself the way you did to me for my life span, and at that, to be monogamous. If you need time to think or—'

'Yes!' James's head shot up – Chad's eyes burned with a primal passion James had only seen on occasion, the passion Chad only showed James. 'Yes, I will turn you.'

James's heart leapt and his stomach flipped a few times.

'I am ready to spend the rest of eternity with the one man whom I love more than I've loved anyone before, the one man who has ignited in me a fire more intense than anyone ever has. I was ready to marry you, wasn't I? I proposed to you, didn't I?'

Chad beamed at James. 'James, you've lit a blaze inside of me that will never be extinguished. I am ready to commit to you for millennia beyond today. For millions of years and aeons if we can manage it. I promise to be yours forever, James, now and beyond all existence. When the world has ended and we continue to live, I will still love you and be solely yours.'

'Chad,' James let out a sob, so happy was he, 'I commit to you for all existence and beyond all space and time as well.'

Chad pounced forward and his lips engulfed James's, his tongue jabbing into James's mouth as he sucked on his tongue. When Chad pulled away, his eyes had paled into their grey-white, and his canines were extended.

'Last call.'

'Ready when you are, baby.' The two men grinned lustily at each other. 'Turn me. Make me yours eternally.'

Chad stood and positioned himself in front of James. He slowly removed James's shirt, which only made the werewolf's anticipation grow. His hyper-awareness made him shiver in excitement as Chad's fingers traced a line on James's skin over a vein. Chad kissed his neck and James let out a soft moan, his husband's breath hot on his neck and already eliciting a throb of arousal in his lap.

James tilted his head, giving Chad better access, and he felt his husband's tongue lick a sensitive part. It made his arousal grow, and his already hard cock pulsed. James was so turned on, he barely felt the sting as Chad's eyeteeth pierced his skin.

James's entire body tingled as Chad sucked on his blood, and James began to feel a vibration coming from within. His claws extended and his eyes flared. And then James felt his canines extend.

Chad closed his lips around James's punctures and James groaned loudly, gripping the bed mattress tightly. As James breathed heavily, both exhilarated and aroused, Chad pulled away, lust in his eyes. James growled in his throat and pulled Chad to him – their canines collided as he kissed him hungrily.

Using his werewolf strength, James flipped Chad over to pin him onto the bed, his hand still on the small of his back, kissing him with lusting passion. Chad panted loudly into his mouth and James growled in response. Sliding himself on his husband, he used his free hand to rip Chad's shirt off. James roared softly as he did so, before lifting himself only long enough to remove his own top.

He tossed this one aside where it landed on the torn shirt. James fumbled at Chad's belt as Chad greedily devoured his face, frantically undoing James's belt. James backed away and jumped to remove his pants in one go and then pulled Chad's boxers off him, ripping them too in the process.

Chad merely moaned as he stared wide-eyed, looking eager for all of James. James grinned, feeling playful, and he plunged his mouth to Chad's balls, engulfing one of them with a soft sucking motion. Chad cried out. James continued, licking his way around the area, while fingering Chad's perineum.

James opened his mouth to half-kiss and half-nibble at Chad's sensitive areas, always licking his way around, and he groaned every time he opened his mouth, enticed by Chad's moans of pleasure the more he did so. Chad arched his back. James grabbed his husband's cock and began to pump him with vigour.

'Oh my god, baby, you're going to make me explode!' cried Chad.

James positioned himself sideways to get a better angle and licked from Chad's perineum to his sack and back. As before, James moaned every time he brought his mouth down again, opening his lips to devour the spots he was licking.

'I feel like I'm making out with your balls!' James groaned as Chad let out a long loud sigh of yearning. James plunged for another mouthful of Chad's delicious package. James felt he was lucky he had found a man who enjoyed the hairy look as well as enjoyed tasting it, and at that, just as much as James did.

James licked up Chad's length and flicked his tongue hard on his shaft.

'Oh my god, James, you're gonna make me come like that.' Chad lifted his head to look at James.

'Then come!' James urged. As he continued – pumping with one hand, fingering with the other, thumbing Chad's balls and licking his shaft – he looked up into Chad's eyes. 'My creator. Come for your werevamp.'

'Oh god!' breathed Chad, his eyes rolling back, and his head slammed onto the bed. He screamed in crescendo layers and spilled onto James's tongue, the warm fluid dripping from James's mouth back onto Chad's cock.

James licked his husband's cum off his dick and lapped up the semen off his pubes, taking his time and savouring it all.

He moved to meet Chad's mouth with his – again, their canines collided, this time a little less forcefully. This would take some getting used to.

'I want you to pump my ass, Chad. I want you to pump it hard!'

Chad gave James a soft push and James brought his legs up and straightened, remaining on his knees. Chad moved to stand on his knees behind James, grabbing onto his broad back and looping his arms around his shoulders. He grabbed James's cock with one hand before James felt him slide into his anus.

'Fuck, yeah!' cried James. 'Fuck, baby, make me come like this.'

James slapped his hands onto the wall, bracing himself for the pleasure that was about to erupt inside his ass.

* * *

Chad pumped James hard, harder than he ever had or wanted to before – and they could be so fucking intense sometimes. The desire of this night fuelled his stamina more than ever before. The way James had looked at him, calling him his creator . . .

'Fuck!' cried Chad. He rubbed his thumb over the tip of James's shaft. 'Stick your fingers into me, James. Baby, I need to feel you in my ass!'

James reached an arm over and did as Chad bade him to.

A dizzy spell hit Chad as the heat of his orgasm rose. Unable to handle the intensity of it, Chad let go of James's cock and squeezed his husband's shoulders hard with both hands. James shouted an, 'Oh fuck,', as Chad's cock stiffened before its eruption.

Chad screamed so loud it echoed throughout the house, his scream was elongated and became hoarser and hoarser as he came harder and harder into James's ass. He thrust again and again before pushing in deep and holding himself there.

Everything became a haze as his vision blurred, unfocused by the intensity of the elation washing through his entire body. Several more pulses made Chad's pelvis and legs jerk as a final spurt spilled from his dick.

Chad sighed loudly, kissing James's back before gently pulling out.

A low guttural growl came from James. 'You're not done with me yet.'

Chad chuckled. 'As if I'd forget you, baby.'

Chad moved with vampiric speed to position himself in front of James and pushed him down onto the mattress. His mouth was on his oozing shaft within seconds, sucking as hard as he could, wanting to swallow James whole, thrusting his husband's plump cock deep into his throat.

'Fuck, baby! Oh my fucking god, Chad! Fuuuuuck!'

James swayed and spasmed as Chad sucked him. His sharp claws grabbed onto Chad's shoulders, digging into his flesh, his flesh that healed instantly.

Chad looked up as he sucked to see that James's teeth had sharpened in werewolf style. Sharp werewolf teeth with two extended canines. Chad lifted his mouth to gape at his husband.

'Fuck, you're so fucking sexy like that.'

And then he thrust two fingers into James's rectum as he plunged his mouth back onto his cock, sliding his canines along the large plumpness that only became harder.

James let out a long growl, bucking his hips upwards to match Chad's movements and speed. And then James jerked his head back. He roared, a true deep and reverberating werewolf's roar that elongated into a scream.

Chad's mouth was filled with the gushing of James's semen, his length so deep in his throat, Chad instinctively swallowed.

'Oh, fuck, baby!' James breathed loudly. 'Fuck!' A few more airy 'fuck's followed as James pulled out of Chad's mouth and joined Chad in a cuddle position. 'Fuck that was amazing.'

'How does it feel to be a werevamp, husband?' asked Chad.

'Oh, it feels fucking amazing. As do you. Oh fuck, baby.'

Chad chuckled as James let out a higher-pitched laugh. The werevamp raked his hand through his hair. 'Fuck,' he whispered.

Chad turned his head to stare at him, amused. He bit his lip enticingly, still aroused by how sexy James was.

'You're a sexy werewolf, James. But you're even sexier as a werevamp.'

'Good, because a werevamp is who I am now and who you'll be staring at and fucking for an eternity.'

'Good!' Chad declared. And they both chuckled.

Chad shifted his position to admire James's were-vamp face. He hovered above James, propped on his elbows. 'James baby, I'm going to love you until the end of time.'

'Chad baby, I'm going to love you until the end of time,' whispered James.

Chad bent and kissed James softly. After the intensity of before, it was nice to simply be tender with each other. He looked forward to spending the rest of time with James by his side.

Chibi Art by Kemvee

<u>More To Come</u>

In the thrilling and sexy sequel,
Ravaging Rapture.

The hunt for Troy is on, as Ian and Rayan follow his scent. Except what they find is a gruesome scene that perplexes as much as it leaves more questions unanswered.

Meanwhile, Rayan must uncover the secrets that this fae's Promised – Rayan's chosen mate and best friend – is hiding from everyone, including the Fae High Council.

ACKNOWLEDGEMENTS

It has been an absolute thrill to follow Chad and James's love story, the struggles their marriage faces with them being a vampire and a werewolf, and the conflicts it forces them to overcome.

Diving into more backstory – with Liam and Julian being integral characters in the couple's journey – and working on Book 2 of this supernatural chronology, gave rise to the series name: *Tenebrārum*, meaning 'darkness,' 'night,' and 'obscurity' in Latin.

Hence, I must thank my friend Cat from one of the writing groups in which I am a member on Discord, who proofread and verified my Latin translations, correcting inconsistencies and ensuring I had the correct declensions in place. I am utterly grateful for the help in smoothing it out.

I, of course, must thank my family and friends, including my husband, who always support my writing and encourage me to pursue these publishing dreams.

Last but not least, I would like to acknowledge my artist, Kemvee, who once again did a phenomenal job with the Chad and James portraits and the cover art. Not to mention that cute Chibi art I included near the end of the book. I am always awestruck at her artwork and her ability to take the descriptions I give her and bring my characters to life with such immense detail.

When I look at her art for Chad and James, I can hear James growl in his throat and Chad reacting in his primal way. A true sensual depiction of our vampire-werewolf husband duo.

Of course, the *Tenebrārum* series has more encores to come, with a hunt underway and secrets in the Fae Realm to unearth. I am eager for you to discover the ravaging rapture that consumes our werevamp 'pup' and 'insipid' fae rivalmance pairing.

<u>Also By Eidahs</u>

The Thief and His Hunter Book 1
The Thief and His Hunter Book 2
(https://binkyproductions.com/thethiefandhishunter)

Sanguine Sincerity
(https://binkyproductions.com/Tenebrarum)

Like Father, Not Like Sons
Legacy Takedown
Of Sullied Dreams and Beaten Hearts
Butchery At the Debauchery
Serendipitous Tribulation
Turbulent Justice
A Romance to Freedom and Pride
(https://.binkyproductions.com/shortstories)

You will find more books
published by Binky Ink at:
https://binkyproductions.com/books

About the Author

Eidahs is a pseudonym for all mature written works, from thrillers to erotic romance. Eidahs in pronunciation sounds elven in nature, which is why she chose it, to tap into her love of fantasy, a genre that couples well with super-natural and preternatural, dark fantasy, and romance.

Eidahs is also the nickname 'Shadie' backwards, repre-senting the shadow self, innermost desires, and a spectrum of emotions, most notably, passion, sorrow, rage, and delight, which Eidahs loves to incorporate in her writing. Enticing readers and evoking the characters' emotions when she writes has guided her inspiration to spell many short stories on Medium and a series of books under this pen name.

Connect with Binky Ink:

WordPress Website & Blog
    https://binkyproductions.com/binkyinkwriting
Medium – Main Profile
    https://medium.com/@BinkyInkWriting
X (Twitter) https://twitter.com/binkyinkwriting
Inkitt: https://inkitt.com/eidahs

www.ingramcontent.com/pod-product-compliance
Lightning Source LLC
Chambersburg PA
CBHW070433120726
47910CB00003B/771